I0659209

Sauntering
VAGUELY DOWNWARD

NESSA L. WARIN

Dreamspinner Press

Published by
Dreamspinner Press
382 NE 191st Street #88329
Miami, FL 33179-3899, USA
http://www.dreamspinnerpress.com/

Sauntering Vaguely Downward

Cover Art by Paul Richmond   http://www.paulrichmondstudio.com

ISBN: 978-1-61372-186-5

Printed in the United States of America
First Edition
October 2011

eBook edition available
eBook ISBN: 978-1-61372-187-2

To Martha, who wouldn't let me not; Alicia, who let me run away with the idea; Elizabeth and Melissa, who poked, prodded, and flailed with me; and Kelsi and Angelica, who introduced me to the wonders of Dragon*Con.

AUTHOR'S NOTE

Sauntering Vaguely Downward is, on some levels, an unabashed homage to my love for Neil Gaiman, Terry Pratchett, and Dragon*Con. The title is a bastardized quote from *Good Omens* by Neil Gaiman and Terry Pratchett, in which the demon Crowley is described as, "An Angel who did not so much Fall as Saunter Vaguely Downwards." The slogan on the T-shirt Brendan is wearing Monday afternoon is also from *Good Omens* and also describes Crowley.

While this story is, obviously, fictional, most of the events mentioned really did happen, and descriptions of them come from my own personal experience at Dragon*Con 2009. That said, all opinions are entirely my own and should not be held to reflect on the convention or its other attendees. I would like to take this opportunity to apologize to the Crossed Swords, who graciously take on the task of emceeing the Friday Night Costume Contest every year, and to thank the celebrities, guests, workers, and volunteers who have made Dragon*Con possible for the past twenty-five years. Having been part of producing one event, I know how much work it is, and I am forever grateful to those who keep doing it.

Descriptions of the hotels, the Peachtree Center, and MARTA are as accurate as I could make them. Likewise for the Dealers Rooms, Exhibit Halls, and Art Show, with the obvious exception of the two inserted vendors. All the other booths mentioned do exist.

Dragon*Con is an amazing time, and I highly recommend that anyone who is into science fiction, fantasy, or pop culture check it out. More information can be found http://www.dragoncon.org.

THURSDAY

DYLAN ROJERS bounces on his toes as he looks down over the railing onto the lobby level of the Atlanta Marriott Marquis. Behind him, the Pulse Lounge is filling up, eager geeks mingling with amused football and NASCAR fans—the ones who heard they could get a good room rate by telling the hotel they were here for the convention and then going to the game or the race anyway. It's always interesting to watch them. Some clearly won't be back next year, while others get a kick out of the Dragon*Con attendees and come back year after year, not just for the price, but also for the entertainment. By Saturday night, they'll be mingling with the con-goers, their lack of a badge the only clue that the jersey they're wearing is for an actual football game or race instead of some video or role-playing game.

It's always fun to watch people arrive to Dragon*Con. The carts pulled by overworked bellhops constantly hold the most interesting things, and it's great fun for Dylan to see if he can spot what someone will be dressing as from the bits and pieces that stick out of their luggage. Wings are big again this year, no surprise there, as are lightsabers and stormtrooper helmets. There have been a few big pieces that Dylan hasn't been able to identify, and twice he's turned to ask Eric if he has a guess, only to turn back, biting down disappointment and trying his best to ignore the nervous twisting in his stomach. Dylan's friend and usual roommate ended up not being able to come this year, so Dylan advertised for and found a roommate online. Now he gets to face the pleasure—and apprehension—of rooming with a total stranger.

Whatever his roommate turns out to be like, it won't really matter in the end. It's not as if Dylan plans to do much more than crash in the hotel room between panels and after the late-night events. It's really more of a place to keep his stuff, and so long as this dontbelieve31 keeps his hands off Dylan's costumes and leatherworking materials and didn't lie about his intentions involving room parties, they'll be good. Dylan doesn't have to like the guy, he just has to collect $450 from him and let him crash in the other bed and use the bathroom.

It'll be easy, and next year Eric will be back—at least he'd better, or Dylan's going to kick his ass, and geek he might be, but that doesn't mean Dylan isn't built—so Dylan doesn't have to worry about making friends with the guy. He can tolerate anyone for five nights.

It's almost time to go down to the lobby level and meet his roommate. Dontbelieve31 had been extremely grateful for Dylan's last-minute post to the roommate communities—apparently his friend had bailed on him at the last minute as well, only he canceled the hotel reservation when he did so—and had been perfectly agreeable to everything Dylan had suggested about meeting up. He'd promised to arrive by two thirty so that Dylan could collect the cash and give him a room key—the Marriott insists on collecting the full amount for the room when the first person checks in during Dragon*Con—and they could head down to the Sheraton in plenty of time to get in line to collect their badges. Dylan has no illusions that they'll be at the front of the line if they don't arrive at the check-in area until three, but he knows better than to wait until four as well. He made *that* mistake the first year he came.

It's now two fifteen, and dontbelieve31 is supposed to be showing up in fifteen minutes. Dylan can't wait to meet him. At the same time, he really doesn't want to at all.

SAUNTERING VAGUELY DOWNWARD

BRENDAN STONE curses as his escape route is cut off by yet another woman gabbing on her cell phone. He swears he has to be the only person who cares at all about getting to baggage claim in a timely manner—not that doing so will be very helpful in the long run. He's still going to be late, and binkysrider719 is going to be angry, he just knows it. The guy had only mentioned about eighteen times how he wanted to be able to get over to the Sheraton by three, and Brendan had promised he'd arrive by two thirty so they would have plenty of time to get his stuff to their room, but it's two twenty, and he hasn't even made it to baggage claim yet.

It's just one more thing he's going to curse his best friend Nate for the next time he sees him. If the asshole hadn't bailed on Brendan at the last minute, canceling their hotel reservation in the process, Brendan wouldn't be so worried about getting to the hotel on time. Of course, if Nate hadn't bailed on him, he wouldn't even be in the Atlanta airport, fighting against crowds of people who apparently flew in to stroll through terminals and have nowhere they need to be at all. They would have driven, and timed it so they'd be arriving just about now, hitting downtown Atlanta in the "lull" between lunch and dinner where they'd only have to slow to about thirty miles per hour on the highway instead of practically stopping.

Brendan had considered looking in the Dragon*Con internet communities for someone to share a ride as well as someone to share a hotel room, but he'd decided against it, and he wasn't about to drive from West Seneca, New York, all by himself. Sharing a hotel room with a stranger is one thing—he doesn't plan to actually use it much. Driving fourteen hours with someone he doesn't know is completely different.

So now he's stuck, watching the seconds tick by on his watch as he tries to get through the crowds of people. With the way his day is going, by the time he makes it to baggage claim, his suitcase will be crushed beneath everyone else's, or worse, he'll get there to discover his suitcase didn't make it to Atlanta at all. His absolute essentials are packed in his carry-on, but his metalworking tools had to be checked—apparently, they pose a security risk in a carry-on—as are all of his costumes. He wasn't able to bring half the things he wanted anyway, thanks to the airline's baggage rules, and he really, *really* doesn't want to have to fight with them to get the little bit he *was* able to bring.

The crowd parts in front of him, and he surges forward, pushing into the space as quickly as he can, no longer caring that he's jostling people with his laptop bag and carry-on. If they're going to get in his way, they deserve to be hit, particularly the ones on the moving sidewalks who don't understand that you stand on the right and pass on the left. It's not a difficult concept, at least Brendan never thought it was until today, but, apparently, no one who flew into Atlanta this afternoon understands. It's a bit ridiculous, really.

By the time he gets to baggage claim, finds his one bag and his guitar, and gets outside, he's just in time to see the Marriott shuttle pulling away. For a brief moment he considers trying to weasel his way onto the Hyatt or Hilton shuttles—they're going to practically the same place, after all—but knowing his luck, he'd end up in some sort of trouble and end up arriving even later. MARTA it is, then.

Joy of all joys. This con is starting out *fabulously.*

DYLAN is about ready to call it quits, leave a message at the desk, and head over to registration. Dontbelieve31 can just wait for him to get his badge at this point—he's forty-five minutes late and it's bordering on preposterous. He hasn't even e-mailed or texted to let Dylan know what's going on, and Dylan sent him all his contact information before he left yesterday morning. It's not as if the guy doesn't know how to get ahold of him.

If this goes on much longer, Dylan is going to lose all his enthusiasm. He's already lost interest in looking at the carts of people checking in, and even the few adventurous souls who are already in costume are barely making him smile. Dylan is definitely giving dontbelieve31 a piece of his mind when—if—he actually arrives.

He's mentally trimming down his planned Dealers Room purchases and reviewing his bank balance just in case the guy does bail on him when a frazzled-looking guy stops in front of him. He's dragging a giant suitcase with one hand and has a guitar case in the other, and he's weighed down by both a laptop bag and a backpack slung over his shoulders. His clothes are rumpled, and he looks like he's going to fall over at any minute, pulled down by the weight of the luggage he's carrying. Dylan's eyebrow twitches as he looks the guy up and down, but he doesn't say anything, just keeps scanning the crowd, hoping that dontbelieve31 will show up.

"Binkysrider?" the guy asks in a voice so faint Dylan can hardly hear him. That's his screen name, though, so he nods and directs his attention back to the guy.

"Dylan, actually, but yeah," he manages to get out before his brain goes off-line. The guy may be rumpled and travel-worn, but he's gorgeous, a few inches over six feet tall with spiked dark-brown hair, warm hazel eyes, and *freckles*. Dylan loves freckles, and if he weren't pissed at the guy for showing up almost an hour late, he'd be delighted. Okay, he's still delighted, but he's pissed, and he's going to hold onto that, because he's sure with the way his luck is going that the guy will be a raging homophobe, or have a long-term girlfriend, or something that will make Dylan's chances with him less than zero.

"Brendan. Uh, dontbelieve31. Sorry I'm late." His words are still soft, but now Dylan can tell that it's mostly because he's trying to catch his breath. "My plane was delayed, the airport was packed, and by the time I got my bags I had missed the shuttle so I took MARTA, and God, *please* don't make me tell you about how that went." He shudders under the weight of his luggage and hitches his backpack higher on his shoulder.

"You could have called or something." Dylan holds out his phone pointedly, deliberately ignoring the lilt in dontbelieve's— Brendan's—voice that's going straight to his groin. He's pissed off, and he's going to *stay* that way. "I've been standing here for almost an hour. I was about to give up and go get in the registration line anyway. I thought you were bailing on me or something."

"Sorry." Brendan winces. "I swear I printed out the e-mail you sent and tucked it in my laptop bag, but I couldn't find it once I was off the plane, and I didn't think to try to pull it up on my phone until I was on the train, only it didn't keep a strong enough signal to get internet." He hitches his backpack again as it starts to slide down his arm and curses. "Sorry. It just really hasn't been my day."

"Yeah, well, I haven't exactly had a blast either," Dylan retorts, though he knows what Brendan went through is worse than just sitting around and waiting. Still, he's tired, frustrated, and now he's going to have to go stand in line for a couple hours with a bunch of strangers as everyone else he even knows who's coming isn't planning on arriving until later tonight and will have to pick up their badges in the morning. Dylan had shuddered when Kelly told him that, but if it makes the girls happy, well, *he's* not the one who will risk missing Friday morning panels. He had hoped that he would click with his roommate and at least have someone to talk to during the long wait, but it doesn't look like that's happening.

Oh well, it's not as if he can't amuse himself. He's done it before.

He turns on his heels before Brendan can reply and stalks back toward the elevators. "Come on. Our room's on eleven."

"Can you—" Brendan starts to say, but Dylan disappears into the crowd before he can finish. The elevators are obvious, and at nearly six and a half feet tall, Dylan is tall enough that he stands out amongst the slowly building crowd. By tomorrow, it might actually be a problem, particularly if people break out the tall costumes, but right now Brendan should have no trouble following, and Dylan isn't going to get roped into helping with his luggage. Not after *that* introduction.

BRENDAN huffs as binkysrider—Dylan, he reminds himself; it's weird to keep calling his roommate by his online handle, no matter how tempting it might be—disappears into the crowd, making a beeline to the elevators at a speed Brendan can't hope to match, especially not with his luggage falling off his shoulders.

Apparently, Dylan is above helping Brendan get it situated so it doesn't fall to the ground on the way to their room, which was all he was going to ask for. It doesn't matter now, though. Dylan's gone, out of sight and earshot, and Brendan is just going to have to make do if he wants to have a chance of getting on the same elevator as the guy.

It turns out to be a good thing that Dylan told him which floor they were on, because by the time Brendan reaches the elevator bay, Dylan is nowhere in sight. And to think, he seemed like such a friendly guy in the few e-mails and LiveJournal comments they'd exchanged.

When the doors to the elevator Brendan finally manages to catch open on eleven, Dylan is leaning against the far wall of the elevator bay, his arms crossed over his chest and his expressive face set into a deep scowl. "Took you long enough." He pushes away from the wall and starts down the hall, only sparing Brendan a cursory glance to be sure he's following. "We're this way."

"I don't control the elevators, you know," Brendan calls after him as he yanks his suitcase out of the elevator, barely making it through the doors before they close on it. "And it's hard to move quickly in a crowd with luggage." His laptop bag falls from his shoulder as he tries to maneuver around the corner, and he growls low in his throat as he stops. "Can you hold on a second? I'm dropping stuff here!"

The sound Dylan makes can only be described as irritated, and the glare he sends Brendan's way could strip paint from the walls. "I would like to get my badge today, you know."

"So would I! But if it's so damn important to you to go *right this minute*, give me my key, tell me what room it is, and go!" Brendan snaps, tugging on the strap of his bag until it's back on his shoulder and digging in it for the money he owes Dylan for the room. "I'll get myself there! I'm sure I can find the room without you leading me like I'm a packhorse."

"Fine." Dylan whirls around and snatches the money Brendan is holding out. He counts it, pulls a card out of his jeans pocket, and slaps it against Brendan's chest. "Room 1128. It's down that way." He jabs a finger toward the far end of the hall and disappears back into the elevator bay.

Brendan barely catches the card before it falls to the ground. "Terrific." At least he has time to rearrange his bags before trekking down the hallway.

The room is more posh than the one Brendan was going to have shared with Nate—they'd been in one of the overflow hotels, not the Marriott—and for all his other obvious faults, Dylan appears to be neat. His suitcases are lined up against one wall, tucked out of the way, and though he's claimed drawers and a bed, the ones reserved for Brendan are left untouched, as is half the closet space. It seems that when Dylan isn't pissed about things no one can control, he's a reasonable guy.

If he'll let that side of himself show this weekend, they might both survive the con.

The bed is soft, and Brendan's bags sink into the down comforter when he piles them on top of it. He's really, *really* tempted to shove them to the floor and curl up for a nap, but he needs to get his badge too. There's a Voltaire concert tonight that he'd like to attend, and he's been considering getting up to go to the Shatner and Nimoy panel first thing tomorrow morning. If he's going to do either, he's going to have to brave check-in while it's open today.

As he's walking down to the Sheraton, Brendan gets a text from his friend Kevin Scott asking where he is and if he wants to meet up for dinner. He sends back a fervent, *GOD YES*, followed by, *Heading to check in*, and continues his journey with a little more spring in his step. Kevin and his wife, Laura, are great listeners and a lot of fun. They'll be the perfect antidote to Dylan, and texting them might keep Brendan sane through the check-in line.

DYLAN sees Brendan when he gets into line at the Sheraton, but he doesn't say anything or draw attention to himself. He's only about three rows ahead of Brendan when they enter the actual winding queue, and he knows that no one would say anything if he were to flag Brendan down and bring him up so they could stand together, but he doesn't.

Instead, he opens his phone, loses three games of Solitaire, and then opens up his Twitter application.

The tweet that he'd sent when he first arrived in the line— *Awesome. Roommate's an ass. Not going to be in the room much this weekend.*—has five replies, most sympathetic, but one telling him to suck it up because he's lucky enough to be at Dragon*Con. He's annoyed by that response for a moment, but then he reminds himself that the sender isn't someone whose opinion he cares about anyway. He or she—Dylan isn't sure—has been jealous ever since he started talking about making concrete plans for this year. The only reason he hasn't blocked the account from following him is that whoever uses it is always good for retweeting his leatherworking links.

Eric apparently hasn't been on Twitter yet, so Dylan exits the application and dashes off a text message, frowning as he tries to walk and type at the same time. The line is almost always moving because someone leaves the front area where they get their badges every few seconds, but the badges are separated by last name, and a long line at one letter group can hold up the whole thing if no one can get by. The result is a strange stop-and-start movement with the line moving anywhere from a few steps to almost an entire queue row before stopping again.

"You're smart," the girl in front of Dylan says when they stop again, startling him away from frowning at the phone as though that will make Eric respond faster. "Bringing your phone, I mean. I didn't think that I'd need to entertain myself since I got here before the line officially opened."

Dylan chuckles at that, his annoyance with Brendan and his impatience with Eric momentarily forgotten. "I've heard rumors that there are times when the line is short, but I've never figured out when that is. Every time I walk by, the line is out the door. I think it dies down once the convention really starts, but it's always packed on Thursday and Friday."

"It's probably one of those 'I'd tell you, but then I'd have to kill you' things," the girl says with a grin. She moves as the line shuffles forward, and for a moment Dylan thinks that maybe he'll be able to go back to frowning at his phone, but she turns to him again once they stop. "So this isn't your first year, then?"

"No. It's my… fifth? I think. No. Sixth." He goes over it again in his head just to be sure, and nods. "I started coming in 2004, and I've been every year. So '04, '05, '06, '07, '08, and now '09." He holds his fingers up as he counts off the years. "Yeah. Sixth."

"Wow. It's uh, it's my first year, in case that wasn't glaringly obvious." She twists her hair around her left index finger and holds out her right hand. "I'm Caitlin, by the way."

"Dylan," he responds. "And, yeah, it was kind of obvious, but that's okay. We love new blood around here."

Caitlin giggles. "I hope you don't mean that literally."

"Oh, jes," Dylan says, using a really bad imitation of a Bela Lugosi vampire movie accent. "Ve vant to suck jour vlood." He leans in, baring teeth that bear no resemblance to vampire fangs at all, and closes the small gap between him and Caitlin.

She giggles and steps back, and Dylan has to break character to stop her from crashing into the group of people ahead of them in line.

"Careful," he says in his normal voice as he grabs her shoulders and pulls her against his chest instead.

"Thanks," she breathes as he steps back and lets her go. "That could have been embarrassing."

"Welcome," he says, pulling his phone back out of his pocket. He hasn't felt it buzz, but he looks anyway, keeping an avid expression and pushing the buttons even when it tells him that there are no new messages or new tweets.

Caitlin quietly moves along with the line while Dylan peers at his phone, quickly reading the new tweets in his timeline, but as soon as he thinks she's going to leave him to stew about Brendan in peace and tucks the phone back into his pocket, she turns around again. "So are you here by yourself?"

"Sort of?" Dylan shrugs. "I came by myself, but I'm meeting people here. You?"

"Oh, I came with friends. I was excited and wanted to register as soon as possible, but they were tired after our flights and wanted to nap first." She giggles, putting her hand over her mouth as she looks behind them at the spiraling queue. "I think they may regret that."

"Yeah." Dylan looks back too and is surprised to find that they're now closer to the front of the line than the back of it. Just a few rows ahead, he can see the Dragon*Con staff pulling people out of line to go up to the letter groupings that don't have anyone waiting at them. Rojers, unfortunately, isn't in one of them. "No kidding." The line shuffles forward and Dylan again tries to distract himself by playing with his phone.

Again, Caitlin doesn't let him. "So, uh, where are your friends?"

It's obvious to Dylan that she's skirting around asking what she really wants to know—why Dylan keeps scowling at his phone, most likely—but he appreciates that she's not pushing him to talk about something he doesn't want to mention. "Um. Not sure. A lot of them aren't arriving until tomorrow."

"Won't the lines be worse then?"

"Yeah." Dylan shrugs. "They're the ones who will have to stand in them, though, not me."

"Yeah, but it means you can't hang out unless you want to wait in line with them." She shudders. "I don't know about you, but once is enough for me."

Dylan nods fervently. "Oh, yeah. I'll be good to go until next year, I'm sure."

"So, what are you going to do until your friends get here? I mean, my friends and I are going to dinner and maybe out into Atlanta some, but that's not much fun by yourself."

"I don't know." Dylan sighs and glances back to where Brendan was. He's not there anymore, or at least he's not where Dylan looks, and he's not inclined to look too hard. "I had hoped to hang out with my roommate, but the guy is apparently a total ass, so that's out."

"Wait." Caitlin looks up at him with wide, astonished eyes as the line moves forward. "You're rooming with someone you don't know?"

"It's more common than you'd think," Dylan assures her, though based on his experiences with Brendan so far, he's no longer sure it's a good idea. "There are communities online dedicated to finding roommates. It makes it easier to go if you can split the cost."

"Really?"

"Yeah. Some people cram as many bodies as they can fit into a room too. I know a guy who once had eight people crashing in his room."

"The hotel lets them do that?"

"They're not supposed to, but if you keep the *Do Not Disturb* sign on the door, how are they going to know?"

"I guess." Caitlin shrugs. "So your friends aren't here yet and your roommate is an asshole. Man, this con is kind of sucking for you so far."

"Thanks for reminding me," Dylan says dryly. "I'd almost forgotten."

Caitlin's hand flies up to cover her mouth. "Oh! Fuck! I'm sorry! I didn't mean to—" She looks up at Dylan apologetically. "You must think I'm such a ditz."

"You're fine." Dylan sometimes forgets that not everyone can handle his occasional sarcasm. He's usually pretty easy-going, so it takes even his friends by surprise. He should have known that Caitlin wouldn't pick up on it. "You've helped, actually."

"Really?" She chews on her bottom lip as she looks up at him.

"Really." He grins. "I haven't had a chance to be annoyed since you started talking to me."

Caitlin smiles. "Good." She rubs at the back of her neck. "Only now I don't know what to say."

Dylan laughs, asks her what her favorite television show is, and the conversation gets rolling again. They don't have very many fandoms in common, but Caitlin's are popular enough that Dylan knows a little bit about their presence at Dragon*Con and he fills her in. He also tells her about the concerts she's sure to want to make it to, the costume contest, and gives her some pointers for surviving the convention.

By the time they separate to go into their respective lines in front of the badge booths, Caitlin is giggling, and Dylan has actually relaxed. He feels good, like he's supposed to feel at Dragon*Con, and when his phone buzzes with a reply from Eric just as he's walking away with his badge and program guide in hand, he completely abandons the rant he'd planned and instead starts talking about how awesome this year is going to be.

And it will. Even if Brendan really is an asshole.

BRENDAN is in a much better mood when he returns to the hotel room hours later. His wait in the registration line wasn't that long, as he lucked out and they were calling for people to come up to the line that included Stone. He got to slip out of line several rows early and was able to meet up with Kevin and Laura for dinner. They ate at Sear, bracing themselves against four days of nothing but the food court and horribly long lines, then headed to the Pulse Lounge, where they drank until Brendan was able to relax and lost the tension that had been building in his neck and shoulders since his plane was first delayed in Buffalo. He's pretty sure that Laura gave him a back rub at one point, but everything after about nine is a blur, so he can't be positive.

The light is off and Dylan is flopped out on his bed, his feet up near the head and his head resting on his crossed arms at the foot. His eyes are open—barely—and the television is showing some show that Brendan doesn't recognize. "Hey," he mumbles when Brendan eases the door shut behind him. "You get your badge?"

It's a vast change from his earlier attitude, and Brendan is too tipsy to question it even if he wanted to, which he doesn't. He's just going to go with it and hope that the new attitude keeps up all weekend. "Yeah. I, uh, got to skip the line when they started calling for my lane. You?"

"I had to wait the whole time, but yeah. I did." Dylan fumbles for the remote, flips off the television, and pushes himself upright. "I, uh…. Sorry about earlier," he says in a rush, running his fingers through his floppy blond hair and looking at Brendan with a sheepish expression. "I was kind of an ass, and I'm not usually, honest. This year just isn't going the way I'd anticipated and it's stressing me out."

Brendan is drunk enough that it's easy to be magnanimous. "It's okay. I should have taken five minutes to find your number and call or text or something." He sits down heavily on his bed and starts attempting to toe off his shoes, which seem unusually attached to his feet. "It probably wouldn't have made me any later, but I just felt like I had to keep moving, you know?" He gives up on the shoes and just lets himself fall backward, his arms flopping outward to span the bed. "Stupid, but, hey. I never claimed to be a genius." He's close, actually, but he doesn't talk about that. He's with fellow geeks, anyway, and most of them are almost as smart as he is, if not smarter.

They're all smarter than he is tonight. He's pretty sure most of them can figure out how to take off their shoes.

Dylan flops back down on his bed, lying the right way this time, and rolls onto his side to look at Brendan, who has lifted his feet into the air and is again tugging at his shoes. "You all right, man?"

Brendan turns his head to the side and grins. He likes this kinder Dylan much better than the one who met him earlier today. "My shoes are stuck on my feet." He tugs ineffectively on the shoelaces again, but they simply dangle down over his face.

"Dude," Dylan says, rolling off the bed and teetering for a minute before practically falling to sit next to Brendan. "Undressing? You're doing it wrong."

For some reason, Brendan finds that to be the funniest thing he's heard in a very long time. His legs fall heavily to dangle off the bed and he starts laughing hysterically, rolling around and clutching his stomach. "You're doing it wrong!"

"Are you drunk?"

"Probably," Brendan admits once he's stopped laughing enough to form words again. "I met a friend and his wife for dinner, and then we went to Pulse and they kept buying me drinks. Said I was tense." He frowns at the last words and tilts his head so he's looking at Dylan sideways. "I'm not *tense*."

"Not anymore, you're not," Dylan says, laughing. "You kind of were earlier, though."

Brendan tips his head farther and draws his knees up. He twists so he resembles a cat lying all convoluted and curled up, his torso twisted one way, his legs twisted another, and his head turned as far as it would go. "Was I?" He blinks as he thinks about that for a minute and then nods decisively. "Guess I was. Sorry." He flashes an apologetic grin. "I'm not usually, really. I just hate flying. And being late. And crowds. And slow people. And riding MARTA. MARTA scares me. Have you ridden MARTA?"

Dylan's expression is growing more amused by the minute. "I park my car at one of the stations up the line and take the train back. That way I don't have to pay for valet parking. It's not that bad if you know where you're going."

"It is with luggage," Brendan declares with a decisive nod. "And the Peachtree Center Station is *horrible*." He draws out the last word, his lips curving around the O for several seconds. "I went out the wrong exit and got lost and had to drag my luggage all around the block before I found the hotel." He reaches out to pat Dylan's knee but hits the bedspread next to him instead. "Don't ever do that. It's not fun. Not even a little bit. Not even any. Not even at all."

"I'll, uh, keep that in mind." Dylan heaves himself up off the bed and looks down at Brendan for a minute, shaking his head and fighting a smile. "If I get your shoes off, do you think you can manage the rest yourself?"

It takes Brendan a few seconds to realize what Dylan is asking, and then he has to seriously think about it. He's not sure that he's coordinated enough at the moment, but there are worse things than sleeping in his clothes, so he nods. "Maybe?"

"That's... not very encouraging." Dylan tugs Brendan's shoes off, hauls him to his feet, and points him in the direction of the bathroom. "Go. And get water while you're in there. You'll need it."

The room is spinning in a way that it most definitely wasn't before Brendan lay down, and he clings to Dylan while he attempts to get his balance. Dylan is firmly muscled beneath his T-shirt, his biceps flexing under Brendan's fingers as he forces Brendan to move, and Brendan doesn't want to let go. He's good right here, with Dylan holding him up and his inhibitions lowered enough that he can stare up at Dylan without feeling ashamed. "You're hot."

"And you're drunk." Dylan walks Brendan to the bathroom, his hands on Brendan's shoulders the whole way. Inside, he fills a glass with water, thumbs open the button on Brendan's jeans, and points him toward the toilet. "Drink the water. And after you use the bathroom, don't put your jeans back on. I'm going to go turn down your bed."

The instructions are simple, but as Dylan closes the bathroom door behind him, Brendan finds himself repeating them aloud as he struggles to puzzle out what they mean. Finally, he gulps the water, slams the plastic cup back onto the counter, and begins peeling off pieces of clothing, one at a time.

When he emerges from the bathroom clad only in boxers, there's a pile of clothing on the floor and puddles of water on the sink. Part of Brendan's brain is telling him that he shouldn't leave a mess like that, especially not while sharing a room with someone he doesn't really know, but he doesn't have the energy or coordination to do anything about it at the moment. He'll fix it in the morning.

The bed is turned down and Brendan wastes no time falling into it, rolling around to get his feet under the covers and then fumbling for the sheet as he buries his face in his pillow. He keeps tugging at something that doesn't move, but then the sheet settles over him seemingly of its own accord, and the light clicks off, plunging the room into near-total darkness with only the light spilling in from the bathroom providing any illumination at all. Something warm pats his head, and he nuzzles at it for a second before letting his head drop heavily back onto the pillow and sighing with relief.

Sleep claims him within seconds.

FRIDAY

A SHRILL, persistent beeping sound wakes Dylan a little more than three hours after he finally falls asleep. He'd been exhausted when Brendan had stumbled in last night, but by the time he'd gotten the other man in bed, he'd been wide awake, and had lain in the dark for nearly an hour before pulling out his booklight and his much-read copy of *Hogfather*.

It had been after two by the time he'd finally shut the book and drifted off to sleep.

Now it's slightly after five, and he's awake again, thanks to that stupid alarm. If it doesn't stop *right now*, he's going to scream. It is far too early to be up.

As a general rule, Dylan likes mornings. He often gets up an hour before he needs to so he can go running with his dogs, and he's the first one to volunteer when work asks for people to come in early. He also likes getting a good night's sleep, however, and he's a big fan of relaxing when he's on vacation, so he's really not happy about being woken up.

Problem is, it's not his alarm that's going off. It's Brendan's, and he's showing no inclination to turn it off. He hasn't moved at all, at least not as far as Dylan can tell when he finally shoves the thick down comforter off his head to peer across the room, and it doesn't look like he's going to, either.

"Brendan!" Dylan is pretty sure that his pitiful early morning croak isn't going to be more effective at waking his roommate than the shrill alarm, but he has to try. Yelling is far preferable to getting out of bed.

Predictably, Brendan doesn't respond, so Dylan fumbles around on the bed until he finds one of the multiple pillows he'd shoved aside when he'd settled in last night, and flings it toward the other bed. "Brendan!"

That gets a response. Brendan makes an exceedingly disgruntled noise and bats blearily at the pillow and the covers until his head finally emerges from the cocoon he'd wrapped himself in not long after Dylan had gotten him into bed. He squints at Dylan, his face the picture of sleepy confusion, and makes an unintelligible noise that Dylan assumes is supposed to be a question.

"Turn off your alarm," Dylan mumbles, pulling the covers back up to his chin. He doesn't have the energy to deal with a bleary, sleepy roommate at the moment.

Brendan blinks for several seconds before his expression clears and he rolls over and slithers over the mound of pillows on his bed to dig in the backpack wedged between it and the wall. After several minutes that stretch out horribly, the beeping of the alarm annoying Dylan more and more with each repetition, he emerges victorious, holding up the phone and squinting at it as he pushes buttons.

Finally, the alarm stops. Dylan sighs, letting his muscles relax as he relishes the peace.

He's almost asleep again when Brendan tosses the pillow back at him. It hits Dylan square in the chest, and he opens his eyes to find that Brendan has rolled over and is now hanging halfway off the bed, looking at him.

It's a comical scene. The phone is on the floor between their beds and Brendan's arm is hanging down so his hand is resting on the carpet nearby. One foot is peeking out from underneath the covers, and his face is smashed against the edge of the pillow-top mattress, giving him a fish-like expression. "I'm sorry," he mumbles, his voice muffled by the white sheets. "I didn't mean to wake you up."

Great. *Now* Brendan is ready to have cordial conversation. Dylan really, *really* wants to pull the covers up over his head and go back to sleep for a few hours, but curiosity wins out and he rolls onto his side so he can see Brendan. "Why is it set so *early*?" There really is no logical reason he can think of to get up this early, especially not today, when the convention doesn't officially start until the afternoon.

"This is when I had to be up yesterday to catch my flight." Brendan yawns and fumbles for his phone. It takes him three tries to get it on the nightstand, and when he does, he lets his arm fall back to dangle toward the floor. He's not any more on the bed than he was before picking up the phone, and Dylan wonders why he bothered. "Left it on because I thought I wanted to go to the Shatner and Nimoy panel." He pauses, rubs at his eyes, and lets his arm drop again. "Think I'll watch it on DCTV instead."

Dylan lifts his head just enough to peer at the clock on the table between their beds. It's five thirty in the morning, and if he's recalling the program correctly, the panel isn't for several more hours. "Why're you gettin' up so early for that? Panel's not until ten."

"'S the only one they're doin' together. I figure it'll fill up fast and I wanted a seat." He wrinkles his nose. "Think I wanna sleep instead."

"Why's it so early, though? The con doesn't even officially start until one." Dylan has been wondering that since he saw the panel on the schedule posted online. It seems like remarkably poor planning to schedule a panel sure to be extremely popular then. "You'd think if they were going to do a morning panel, it'd be on Saturday."

"Yeah, well…." Brendan rolls onto his back and snuggles down under the covers. He looks absolutely endearing with his freckles standing out in the dim light and his hair spiking in every direction. "Thursday is the new Friday, so I guess that makes Friday the new Saturday."

Brendan isn't the first person Dylan has heard say that, and he shakes his head every time. "Crazy, man. Having stuff Thursday night and early Friday. If they're gonna do that, they ought to just make it officially a five-day con."

"Mmhmm."

When Dylan looks over again, Brendan is asleep, his chest rising and falling in a steady motion. Sending up a quick thank-you to whatever power happens to be listening, Dylan rolls over and snuggles down himself. He'd thought about going to that panel too, but watching it on DCTV is a brilliant idea, now that he thinks about it. He'll catch it then, if he's up. If not, there's always the Internet.

IT'S ten thirty by the time Brendan wakes up again. The room is still surprisingly dark—the blackout curtains are pulled and the lights are off—but he can see that the other bed is empty and hears the patter of the shower through the wall. The last bits of moisture vanish from his already dry mouth when he pictures Dylan naked under the hot spray, and he spends a minute thinking about his grandmother and the guy he'd seen picking his nose on the train yesterday before he dares to move. He does *not* want to think of his admittedly attractive asshole of a roommate that way. It's just going to make things more complicated.

When he finally rolls over, he sees a tall glass of water sitting on the nightstand. Next to it are two red pills acting as the eyes in a smiley face drawn on a piece of hotel stationary. The note scrawled beneath it reads, *Thought you might need these.*

Brendan smiles and picks up one of the pills, examining it until he sees the word Tylenol printed on the glossy surface. They're coated caplets, not gelcaps, so after making sure the other one says the same thing, he pops them into his mouth and washes them down with a gulp of water.

It's the best water he's ever tasted—or more likely he's just *that* thirsty—and he downs the entire glass before he even realizes that he hasn't put it down yet. Apparently, Dylan knew more about how Brendan would be feeling than Brendan did, and maybe he's not as much of an asshole as he'd seemed at first.

At this point, Brendan is pretty sure he's going to end up watching the Shatner and Nimoy panel on the Internet if he watches it at all, but DCTV makes better background noise than anything else that might be playing right now, so he flips through the channels until he finds it and then sets about figuring out his day while William Shatner and Leonard Nimoy banter and take questions from excited fans in the background.

Only at Dragon*Con.

Dylan comes out of the bathroom while Brendan is staring into the dresser drawer, contemplating the merits of jeans and a T-shirt versus one of the costumes he brought. He looks up, ready to smile in greeting and thank Dylan for the water and Tylenol, but stops short as soon as his eyes land on the other man. Dylan is dressed all in black, a skintight T-shirt stretched across his impressive chest and pants that are baggy through the legs but show off the curve of his ass perfectly when he turns. They're both painted front and back with bones so that the effect is that of a full skeleton, but Brendan doesn't really notice that. He just notices how *good* Dylan looks.

Fortunately—or not, now that Brendan thinks about it—Dylan doesn't notice Brendan staring. He just shoves his dirty clothes into his suitcase and grins. "Hey! You're up!"

"Uh, yeah." Brendan rubs the back of his neck and fights back a blush. "Uh, thanks for the Tylenol. And the water."

"No problem." Dylan's smile grows impossibly wider, and Brendan is left feeling like someone found a hidden light switch and flipped it up to brighten the room. He could probably turn all the other lights off with how bright Dylan's smile is. "I figured you'd be thirsty when you woke up and, well," Dylan says with a shrug, "I was right about still being in the shower when you did. You feeling okay now?"

Brendan is still working on getting his brain back online, so he gapes for a minute before he manages to process what Dylan is saying and nod. "Yeah. Just a little headache, but it'll go away once the Tylenol kicks in."

"Good." Dylan pulls a long, black, hooded robe from the closet and slips it on over his skeleton outfit as he peers down into the dresser drawer Brendan has open. "Aren't you wearing a costume?"

He had been leaning toward jeans and a T-shirt, as he knows that they'll be much more comfortable at the end of the day, but when Dylan asks, he's left with no option and shoves the drawer shut. "Yeah, I think I am." Now he just has to pick which one.

It's much harder than it should be to ignore the niggling worry that Dylan won't like it.

Dylan heads back into the bathroom and emerges a moment later carrying his toiletries bag. "Figured I'd do the makeup for this while you shower." He gestures down his body, indicating his costume.

Brendan looks at him curiously. "Do I even want to know?"

"A skull?" Dylan gives Brendan a look like that answer should have been obvious, and rolls his eyes in exasperation when Brendan's confused look doesn't clear. "I'm Death! From the *Discworld* books!"

"Oh! Right!" It takes a few more seconds for the reference to fully penetrate Brendan's sleep-muddled brain, but when it does, he completely gets it. "I've read a few of those. They're pretty good."

"Pretty good?" Dylan looks unnaturally offended by Brendan's positive opinion on the series. "Only *pretty good*?"

"Um… yeah?" Brendan starts backing slowly away, wondering if it's too late to find a new roommate. The one he has is clearly insane. "I picked up a few after I read *Good Omens*. They were entertaining."

"Pretty good? Entertaining?" Dylan sucks in a deep breath and looks as though he's struggling to control himself. "Are you nuts? They're *awesome*! Terry Pratchett is a genius!"

Brendan isn't sure he'd go that far. He'd liked them, sure. They were funny and clever and he'd definitely read more given the opportunity, but they didn't compare to Neil Gaiman's level of genius. Not that anyone actually does, but still. "He's pretty awesome," Brendan concedes, mostly just to keep the peace. "Obviously he has something going for him or Gaiman wouldn't have worked with him on *Good Omens*."

"Wait." Dylan drops his toiletries bag on the desk and whirls to face Brendan. "You think Neil Gaiman is better than Terry Pratchett? Really?"

"Yeah." Brendan takes a step forward, his fists clenched at his sides as he prepares to defend his favorite author. "He's incredible. I mean, have you read *American Gods*? And the *Sandman* books. He's brilliant. Pratchett is good, but all he writes is *Discworld*."

"*Nation. The Bromeliad Trilogy*. The *Johnny Maxwell* books." Dylan takes a step forward with each word, and when he stops, he's standing toe to toe with Brendan. "He writes more than just *Discworld*. Besides, you know his parts of *Good Omens* were the best."

"Excuse me?" Brendan tilts his chin up so he's looking straight into Dylan's eyes. He's not used to people being taller than he is, and it's a little disconcerting, but he's not going to back down now. Not with this at stake. "*Pratchett's* parts of *Good Omens* were the best? You mean the footnotes? And maybe…." Brendan lets his gaze roam up and down Dylan's costume as he twists his lips into a sneer. "Death? You *know* Crowley was all Gaiman."

Dylan makes a noise that could only be described as a snort. "Yeah, right. Pratchett did more of the writing for it."

"Only because Gaiman was obligated to work on *Sandman*." Brendan clenches his fists tighter and huffs. He really, *really* wants to punch Dylan right now, but he's still got just enough common sense left not to, so he focuses on making his words as biting as possible. "Besides, they've both admitted that at the time it made more sense for Pratchett to be the main writer. Gaiman would have been if they'd done it as a graphic novel."

"Well, if you know that, you know that the only thing Gaiman can claim full credit for is the maggots."

"And the only thing Pratchett can claim full credit for is Agnes!"

"Agnes is better than maggots!"

"Is not!"

"Is too!"

They both move at once, shoving at the other. Brendan staggers backward, hits the corner of Dylan's bed, and sits down hard, while Dylan ends up flailing wildly and narrowly misses the television as he struggles to keep his balance. He looks like he's trying to launch into flight, his loose robe serving as wings, and when he whirls his arm up over his head and makes a distressed noise, Brendan can't help but laugh.

It starts low and quiet as he tries to keep it repressed and not further antagonize his roommate, but then Dylan leans forward, his arms still windmilling, and Brendan loses it. A loud guffaw breaks free and he falls back flat onto the bed, pulling his knees up to his chest as he rolls onto his side.

"What's so—" Dylan starts, and then he falls forward, catching himself with his hands on either side of Brendan and his nose just inches from Brendan's hip. He mutters a curse under his breath and pushes himself back to sit on his heels, glaring at the bed and Brendan and everything else in the room. "It's not funny."

"Yeah—" Brendan has to gasp for breath after just that one word; he's been laughing so hard. "Yeah, it kind of is."

"How?"

Brendan struggles into a sitting position and gives Dylan an incredulous look. "We almost came to blows arguing over a book we both love and authors we both like. What isn't hilarious about that?"

Dylan tilts his head to the side, his eyes going fuzzy for a minute, and then he nods, his lips slowly curling upward into one of his room-brightening grins. "Well, when you put it that way...."

They both end up overcome by giggles after that.

It's at least ten minutes later by the time Brendan manages to heave himself off the bed and grab his costume from the closet so he can put it on after his shower. He leaves the boots and coat where they are, but the breeches, vest, and flowing shirt come in with him. As he's about to shut the door, he sees Dylan giving him a curious look, and he grins. "Tristran. From *Stardust.*"

"You mean Tristan?"

"No. Trist*ran*. They changed it for the movie. It's Tristran in the book." Brendan flushes a little, and he has to remind himself not to duck his head or rub at the back of his neck in embarrassment. This is Dragon*Con, the one place he doesn't have to be embarrassed about how geeky he is. "I, uh, like the movie, but I love the book."

Dylan frowns thoughtfully and nods. "I only saw the movie. Never read the book. I meant to, but I never got around to it."

"I have it with me if you want to borrow it while we're here." The words leave Brendan's mouth before he remembers that he probably shouldn't admit to liking a young-adult romantic fantasy enough that he brought it with him to Dragon*Con.

"That'd be great." Dylan smiles his thanks and then his eyes light up mischievously. "It's your favorite Gaiman book, isn't it?"

"Second favorite." This time, Brendan can't stop himself from ducking his head to hide the deepening flush that's spreading across his cheeks and up to his ears. He can feel his skin burning and he's sure that Dylan's going to laugh him out of the room at any minute. "*American Gods* is my favorite, but *Stardust* is second." He looks up with wide eyes. "You can't tell anyone, though. I'll deny it if you do. Everyone thinks my second favorite is *Sandman.*"

"Don't worry." Dylan's eyes are sparkling with amusement and his lips keep twitching, but to his credit, his voice is calm. "I won't, so long as you don't tell anyone that after the Death and Watch books, I like the Tiffany Aching books the best."

"Wait." Now Brendan is having trouble keeping back his laughter again. "Isn't she the teenage girl witch?"

"Well, to be fair, all the witches are women. It's part of the definition of witch in Discworld." Dylan tries to shove his hands into his pockets but is thwarted by his robe, so he just ends up rubbing them against his thighs and looking ridiculous. "But yeah," he continues, clenching at the robe with both fists, "Tiffany is the teenager."

"That's...." Brendan has to struggle to find the word, because really, he can't say anything, not when he just admitted his love for *Stardust*. "Kind of awesome, actually." To his surprise, he actually means it.

Dylan blushes a little. "Thanks. I think. I'll, uh, let you get your shower." He turns toward the desk and Brendan has the door almost shut when he spins back around. "Hey! What are your plans for this afternoon?"

"Food?" Brendan shrugs. "I want to check out that live-action quest thing, see what it's about, and, um, probably hit the Dealers Room so I'll know how much I need to starve myself this weekend to afford what I want."

Dylan's laugh echoes through the small room. "Yeah. Me too." He ducks his head and shuffles his feet a bit awkwardly. "Uh, I'm supposed to meet up with my friends Kelly and Sabrina, but we're pretty much doing exactly that. You're welcome to come, if you want." He looks up before Brendan can reply and barrels on, his eyes wide and his mouth moving at a rapid pace. "I mean, unless you have someone else you're meeting. I'm sure you know someone here, right? You have to, or you wouldn't have come. So, uh, yeah, just ignore me."

"I'm pretty sure Kevin is spending the afternoon with his wife, and Tim and Matt aren't arriving until this afternoon, so… if you mean it, sure."

"Great."

Brendan returns Dylan's smile, and as he shuts the door to the bathroom, it occurs to him that he shouldn't be so thrilled to have elicited it.

DYLAN bounces on his toes as he waits for Brendan to finish putting the final touches on his costume. He looks good—*really* good—in his breeches, boots, vest, and long tailored coat, and it makes Dylan feel like he looks horrible. Which is really kind of the point of his costume—Death isn't supposed to be pretty—but Brendan's costume is so put together that Dylan feels like his is a bit slapdash. Brendan even has a sword—and really, Dylan should not follow his mind down that path—and it's far superior to Dylan's scythe. Of course, swords can be peace-bound while there is no easy way to secure a scythe so it can't be used, which means Dylan is stuck with a fake weapon while Brendan has a real one.

That's really not the point, though. The point is that Brendan looks awesome, while Dylan looks like, well, Death. He does have a little skeletal rat with a robe and scythe perched on his shoulder, though, which makes up for a lot. Death of Rats is made of win.

When Brendan finishes securing his belt, he turns, spreads his arms, and poses. "How do I look?"

Dylan doesn't need the time to look Brendan over again—he's been doing nothing but since he came out of the bathroom—but since it's being offered, he takes it, letting his eyes rake up and down Brendan's body a few times. Brendan is well toned, and his firm muscles fill the costume perfectly, and damn does Dylan need to keep his mind on track if he's going to survive the convention. "They should have had you play Tristran in the movie."

Brendan blushes, the color spreading out to his ears and down his neck. "Hardly," he protests, sticking his room key in his pocket and securing his badge to his belt. "I can LARP well enough, but I'm not that good of an actor."

"You LARP?" Dylan makes sure he has his own badge and room key and leads the way out. "You doing any here?" The idea of Brendan dressing up and running around playing a character as part of a Live Action Role Playing game is oddly appealing and actually piques Dylan's interest in participating. He's never tried out any of the games at Dragon*Con because he's not convinced that there can really be enough of a story for him to truly enjoy the game in such a short time, especially if he wants to do other things at the convention, but if Brendan has joined one, he might just follow along to check it out.

"Not this year." Brendan shrugs. "I wanted to, but I couldn't fit the costumes I wanted into my luggage. Maybe next year I'll drive again and be able to try some then."

"Why didn't you drive this year?"

"'Cause Nate bailed on me. I didn't want to drive from Buffalo by myself." Brendan shudders dramatically at the thought as he pushes the elevator call button.

"Why not?" Dylan grins, thrilled that his roommate is a fellow New Yorker. "I drove from Albany by myself."

"You're from Albany?"

"Born and raised." Dylan puffs out his chest proudly. His reflection in the elevator doors looks ridiculous—the skull makeup stretched by his too-wide grin and his robe hanging weirdly as he poses, exposing the black slipper socks he painted with foot and toe bones—but he doesn't care. He's having fun.

The elevator dings, and as they step inside, Brendan leans in conspiratorially. "Y'know, I'm pretty sure my brother would tell me I'm supposed to hate you because you're probably a Jets supporter."

Dylan wrinkles his nose. "They're football, right? Yeah, no."

Brendan laughs, the sound filling the elevator and making something warm curl in Dylan's belly. "Me neither. As far as I'm concerned, the Bills are lucky I know they're Buffalo's football team. I only know about the Jets because my brother hates them and he'd throw a fit every time they won a game. Man, was I glad when he moved out."

"And you haven't?" Dylan keeps his tone teasing, but there's a part of him that's genuinely curious. This is geek heaven, after all, and while Brendan doesn't look like the kind of guy who's still living in his mother's basement, you never can tell for sure. Dylan's learned that one the hard way.

"Well, yeah, now, but he's four years older than I am, so he moved out first." Brendan nudges Dylan's elbow as he steps out of the elevator. "You thought I lived in my mom's basement, didn't you?"

"No!" Dylan shifts guiltily as he starts to lead the way over to the Peachtree Center, where he promised to meet Kelly and Sabrina. "Well, the possibility crossed my mind, but I didn't really think you were. Not really."

"Uh-huh." Brendan sounds like he could be pissed off, but the grin he throws Dylan as they turn onto the bridge connecting the two Marriott towers is teasing, and Dylan breathes a sigh of relief.

"I'm just glad my older brother never got all that much into it. Some of his friends did, though. Man, was that nuts."

"I know, right?" They stop to let a girl in a boxy costume pass through the doors and head into the second tower. "It's ridiculous how upset people get about it!"

"Exactly!" Dylan would say more, but the bridge leading from the Marriott to the Peachtree Center food court is packed, and they're forced to walk single file. His hooded robe makes it nearly impossible to have a conversation with someone behind him, and at this point, he has to keep an eye out for the girls, anyway.

SAUNTERING VAGUELY DOWNWARD

They see him as soon as they pass the ATM. Dylan shakes his head sadly at the line of people and has just enough time to wonder how long it will take to run out of money this year before he's attacked by a five-foot-two version of Coraline, blue hair streaming out behind her as her rain boots squelch against the linoleum floor.

"Dylan!"

BRENDAN scans the food court, his hands clenched around his Chick-fil-A bag. Dylan and his friends had headed off other places— the girls to Subway and Dylan to wander while he made a decision— but now they had to meet up again, which wasn't exactly an easy prospect. The food court isn't as crowded as it will be on Saturday and Sunday, but it's packed enough, and they're going to have to grab a table where they can find one. There aren't any that Brendan can see, but then again, he can't see Dylan, Kelly, or Sabrina, either. There are just too many people.

It's amazing, really. Until he started looking, Brendan never would have guessed that someone as tall as Dylan in a black cowl and carrying a scythe could blend in *anywhere*, but apparently they've found the one place that he can.

Once he's almost certain that none of them are in the North food court, he heads to the south side, cutting through behind Chick-fil-A and keeping his eyes open as he navigates through the crowd. He spots a table at the same time he sees Kelly, and they both run toward it, eager to claim it before anyone else does. Brendan gets there just ahead of a guy wearing an Imperial Guard uniform, and he shrugs apologetically as he confirms that he does need all four of the chairs. Kelly joins him a second later, sliding into the chair across from him with a grin and tossing her messenger bag on one of the other open seats.

"So," she says, sliding her sandwich out of the plastic bag, "you're the poor sap Dylan found to room with him."

There really isn't a good way to respond to that. "Uh. I guess?" Brendan shrugs as he pulls his chicken fingers and waffle fries from the bag. "I mean, I am rooming with him, so, yeah?" He's not really sure what she means by poor sap, and he's honestly afraid to ask.

She just laughs, the bell-like sound soft but clear, even in the din of the food court. "Don't worry. Dyl's not *that* bad." She grins at him as she unwraps her sandwich. "He hasn't gotten pissy with you, has he?"

"Uh. Yesterday," Brendan admits. "I was late meeting him, and he wasn't in a very good mood when I finally got here." He pauses to pop a fry into his mouth, but once he's swallowed it, honesty compels him to continue. "I wasn't really in a very good mood then, either, though, so I can't really blame him. And we've been fine today. I wouldn't be here otherwise."

"You mean you weren't just dying to meet me?" Kelly puts a hand over her heart and swoons dramatically. "I'm hurt!"

"I haven't heard anything about you," he admits with a wry smile. "Dylan just mentioned your name when he invited me along."

"That brat! He knows he's supposed to extol my virtues every time my name comes up!" She winks, making it clear to Brendan that she's joking, but he's still not sure how to respond, and he just sits there with his mouth open and his mind racing.

He's saved by Sabrina's arrival.

"Ignore her," she says as she circles the table. She bumps the back of Kelly's chair with her hip as she passes and winks at Brendan. "She's desperate for attention."

"Am not." Kelly crosses her arms and shoots a dirty look at Sabrina. Her pout combined with her costume—a yellow raincoat, yellow galoshes, blue jeans, and a bright blue wig with a bow in it— and her diminutive stature make her look remarkably like the child she's dressed as.

Brendan looks away, focusing on Sabrina instead, because, honestly, it's a little weird. It's remarkably cool at the same time, but weird nonetheless.

Sabrina shakes her head and rolls her eyes as she squeezes into a seat. It's an awkward fit with her long, flowing dress and wings that get in the way of everything. She has the kind that are mostly flowing fabric hanging off stiff wires that curve up from her shoulder blades, so they're better than some of the others Brendan can see, but they're still inconvenient. They don't hit the chair back, which means she can sit down without taking them off, but they do stick out behind her, and the wires pull awkwardly when she sits on the free-flowing fabric, so it takes her a few tries to get settled properly.

"I thought you were getting Subway," Brendan comments once she's settled and starts opening her Dairy Queen bag. He doesn't particularly care, but someone has to say something, or the awkward silence that descended while Sabrina was getting settled will drive him away before Dylan makes it to the table.

"I was, but"—she shrugs and smiles sheepishly—"I decided I wanted french fries instead. Not exactly the most healthy choice, but if you can't indulge when you're on vacation, when can you, right?"

"Amen," Kelly agrees. Her lips twist up into a smile when she sees Brendan's pointed look at the Subway bag. "I got a Chicken Bacon Ranch. It's not exactly the healthiest thing on their menu. Besides, I like it."

"If you say so." Brendan swirls some chicken into his honey and pops it into his mouth. It's delicious, and, as always, he finds himself wishing he could eat at Chick-fil-A more often. "Have either of you seen Dylan?" he asks once he's swallowed. "I wouldn't think a guy his size could get lost, even in this crowd, but...." He trails off, shrugging as he looks around again.

"He is amazingly good at disappearing," Sabrina agrees. "He'll find us, though. He's good at that too. Plus, these wings aren't exactly inconspicuous. I don't exactly blend in."

"Like you could ever blend in anywhere." Dylan slides into the remaining open seat, almost sitting on Kelly's messenger bag. She barely manages to snatch it away before he settles in the chair, propping his scythe against the table so it looms over Kelly's head, and opens his container from Tropical Cajun.

"You're one to talk," Sabrina shoots right back. "You're a giant dressed as a skeleton and carrying a scythe. How is it that I'm the one who doesn't blend in?

"I'm not nearly as beautiful as you are." Dylan makes a kissing face across the table at Sabrina as he spears a piece of meat on his fork. "Why would anyone notice me when you're around?"

Sabrina rolls her eyes. "You know, you're a lot more charming when you're not dressed like the Grim Reaper."

"You love me anyway."

"Yeah, right. Besides, you're not interested, remember? If there's anyone at this table you're interested in, it's Brendan, not me."

Brendan freezes as all three sets of eyes land on him. It's disconcerting, and while their banter was mildly amusing when they were directing it at each other, he finds he doesn't really want to be the center of attention, especially not when something like *that* was just revealed. This is not the time or the place he wanted the revelation that the guy he's rooming with—and crushing on—is gay.

His face flames up, the blush spreading out to his ears and down his neck, burning his skin far below the open neck of his shirt. He ducks his head to hide it, his hand rubbing at the back of his neck as he tries to get his brain back online. All he can think is that this is the worst possible place to have gotten that information. There's no way he's going to be able to act on it or even brush it off, not with Kelly and Sabrina watching, and now he's going to look like an idiot, and Dylan's going to think he's an asshole again, and they're both going to spend the rest of the convention uncomfortable in each other's presence.

"I, uh." Brendan tries to look up and meet Dylan's eyes. He really wants to just blow this off, to laugh at it and show that he's not bothered, so that later he can let Dylan know *why* he's not bothered, and maybe they can both have a little extra fun this weekend, but his mouth won't work. He can feel three sets of eyes on him, waiting for him to say something, but he can't. Brendan's comfortable with his own sexuality, and he's not exactly in the closet—his family, friends, and coworkers all know, and he doesn't try to hide it—but he's not flamboyantly out either, and he likes to keep his hook-ups and relationships discreet, at least at first. The mere idea of doing anything, even harmless flirting, with Kelly and Sabrina right there has his stomach coiling in terror.

"I have to go," he finally manages, grabbing his food as quickly as he can and refusing to meet any of their eyes. He still has over half his meal left, but he can't eat it now, and he shoves it into the nearest trash can before fleeing the food court, his hand fumbling in his bag for his phone as he dashes back over the bridge to the Marriott.

DYLAN'S heart sinks as he watches Brendan run off. He knew that this was a possibility, which was why he'd intended to just keep his sexuality private—it's not like he needs to hook up this weekend—and Sabrina had to go and ruin it. "Thanks, Sabrina," he says, glaring at her with narrow eyes once Brendan has disappeared into the crowd, "Really. I wanted to be uncomfortable in my hotel room this weekend."

"I'm sorry." Sabrina sets her food down and ducks her head, a faint blush staining her cheeks as she chews on her bottom lip. "I didn't know."

"Would it have killed you to keep your mouth shut?"

"I'm *sorry*," she repeats, more emphatically this time. "I wasn't thinking, okay?"

"Dylan, come on." Kelly lays a hand on his arm. "She didn't mean anything. It was an accident." She shrugs and tucks a bit of stray hair under her wig before continuing. "At least you know?"

"And what good does that do, Kelly?" Dylan drops his fork with a sigh. He wants to rub his hand over his face or push his hair back, but he's trained himself to be completely aware of his costume and makeup, and since he *really* doesn't want to go back to the room right now to try to fix it, he doesn't dare do anything that might mess it up. "We're stuck rooming together for the rest of the weekend. It's not like I can avoid him."

"You could ask him to leave?"

"And where exactly would he stay? We're not exactly rooming together because we're BFFs. He's there because he doesn't have anyone else to room with." He lets his head fall forward, making sure his hands hit the cowl rather than makeup when they catch it. "Besides, I can't afford that room by myself."

"He's the one who has a problem with it." Sabrina pushes her fries around in her box before pulling one out and holding it between two slender fingers. "If he really can't stand it, maybe he'll end up finding someplace else to go. And if he doesn't, just ignore him." She pops the fry into her mouth with a shrug.

"Yeah, I guess." Dylan picks up his fork and starts pushing his food around his plate. The chicken and rice doesn't look nearly as appetizing as it did when he'd purchased it, but he dutifully shoves a forkful into his mouth anyway. Kelly will yell at him if he doesn't eat, especially since the first time they'd all gone to Dragon*Con he'd forgotten one day and ended up passing out due to low blood sugar. He's secretly convinced that she has never forgiven him for making her miss the Voltaire concert, and she harps to make sure it doesn't happen again, but she has a point, regardless of her reasons, and so he listens. Most of the time.

Kelly squeezes his arm before picking her sandwich up again. "It'll work out, Dylan. You'll see. Maybe he'll avoid you, and you'll basically get the room to yourself for half the cost." She grins as she shoves the sandwich into her mouth, ripping through the bread and pulling a whole tomato slice out when her teeth fail to fully cut through it.

Dylan manages a small smile as he forces his food down his throat. "Maybe," he agrees between bites, more because he doesn't want to talk about it anymore than because he actually believes that it will happen. Whether she knows of his subterfuge or not, it works, and conversation turns to their plan of attack on the Dealers Room and Exhibit Hall as they finish their lunch. Dylan says far less than usual, but Kelly and Sabrina don't point it out, and by the time they vacate their table to an anxiously hovering group of people dressed as Ravenclaws and Gryffindors from *Harry Potter*, it's starting to feel like an almost normal afternoon again.

BRENDAN dashes in front of the blood-donation area, shaking his head at the Life South volunteers and clutching his phone to his ear as he desperately prays for Kevin to answer. His first instinct is to run and hide in the room, but Dylan might go there, and Brendan needs to get his head on straight before he risks encountering Dylan again. He messed up by leaving, he knows he did, and he has to figure out how to fix it, and quickly.

If it's even fixable.

Kevin answers just as Brendan gets over to the other side of the Peachtree Center towers. He doesn't make it very far in, but he doesn't need to. It's amazing how much quieter it is only a few feet away from the bustle and flow of the crowd. He can hear Laura clearly in the background when Kevin answers the phone, and he's immediately assailed by another wave of guilt. They'd planned an afternoon together, and now Brendan is interrupting it. "Sorry," he says in response to Kevin's greeting. "I forgot you had plans."

"It's fine." Kevin waves off his concerns. "We aren't quite ready to head out yet. What's up?"

"I'm an idiot." Brendan can almost see Kevin's surprised look as he blunders on, catching him up on what had happened with Dylan that morning and how they were almost becoming friends, and then how Brendan completely messed the whole thing up by freezing and then fleeing at lunch. "It's stupid, and I know it was stupid. I just couldn't think, and then I was moving before I realized what I was doing, and it didn't even occur to me what he must think now until it was too late to turn around." He sinks down to the floor, his back to the wall, and lets his head thud back against the plaster.

"So apologize tonight. Earlier if you can find him. You could go back to the food court and tell them why you ran." They both know that Brendan isn't going to do that, and the knowledge shows in Kevin's tone. "Or go find him. You know where he's going this afternoon, right?"

"Dealers Rooms," Brendan replies in a flat tone. If he finds Dylan there, it'll be a miracle.

"Okay." Kevin draws the word out. "That eliminates calling him too. With your luck, he doesn't get a signal in there."

"Thanks." Sarcasm drips from the word.

"I try. Seriously, though, just catch him at the earliest opportunity and explain. He might still think you're an idiot, but at least he won't worry that you're going to trash his stuff or start preaching at him."

"Yeah." Brendan sighs. He knows Kevin is right, but that doesn't mean that he's looking forward to the conversation.

"Try not to stress too much, okay? And give Tim a call. He texted me about twenty minutes ago and said that he and Matt are at the Hyatt. They ought to be checked in soon."

Brendan shudders at the thought of venturing into the Hyatt lobby, but he can't keep Kevin on the phone all afternoon, and he isn't ready to go hide in his hotel room. His mood has been killed, but he won't fix it by moping around. Tim Ayers and Matt Blackburn might be the perfect antidote. They'll tell him what an idiot he is and bemoan the fact that he didn't jump Dylan right there in the food court—they're that sort of demonstrative couple—but then they'll have stories that will take Brendan's mind off the entire thing. At the very least, they'll keep him entertained while he gathers the courage to go face Dylan again. "I will," he agrees, a genuine smile slowly blooming on his face. "Thanks."

"You're welcome." Kevin covers the phone, says something to Laura, then unmuffles it. "I gotta go. Are we still filking tonight?"

At the moment, Brendan isn't in the mood to sit in public with his guitar, playing and singing geeky songs and science-fiction-inspired parodies, but the sessions are often the highlight of his convention, and he knows he'll regret it if he doesn't go. "That's the plan."

"Sweet."

They arrange to meet in the Hyatt later, and Kevin hangs up, leaving Brendan sitting on the floor in the hallway, his phone cradled in one hand and his costume probably getting far dirtier than he'd planned for. He texts Matt and Tim, waits for a response, and then pushes himself to his feet, tucks his phone back into the bag on his belt, and brushes the dirt from his costume. Once he looks as presentable as he's going to get, he takes a deep breath and heads to the escalators.

If he's going to the Hyatt right now, he's not cutting through the food court.

BRENDAN is sitting cross-legged on his bed when Dylan returns. His boots are on the floor next to the wall and his jacket and sword have been laid across one of the pillows, but he still has the rest of his costume on. His shirt is wrinkled, there are streaks of dust along his pants, and he clearly hasn't been there long as the bed is still neatly made under him. He thumbs the remote when Dylan crosses to his own bed, turning off the television. "Hey."

"Hi." Dylan keeps his words short and clipped and he refuses to look at Brendan as he sets about putting away the few small things he bought in the Dealers Room. He's saving the major purchases for later, after he's cased all three rooms several times, but he couldn't resist a new set of dice and a leather bag to keep them in. They didn't cost much and he'll find some sort of use for them, even if it's just decorative. He's glad for them now, as they give him an excuse to stay busy and not talk to his roommate.

Dylan had really been hoping that Brendan would be out of the room when he stopped in, and he's more than a little upset to see him sitting there, chewing on his bottom lip as he watches Dylan tuck away the dice and dig for his program bag. "I'm not going to jump on you, you know," he finally snaps, tired of the spot between his shoulder blades tingling under Brendan's gaze. "You don't have to watch me every second. I promise, your virtue is safe."

"What?" Brendan is blinking when Dylan turns around, and he looks even more confused than he sounds. "I don't think you're going to—" He cuts himself off, shaking his head and sighing. "Can we talk for a minute? Please?"

Talking to Brendan is the last thing Dylan wants to do, but Brendan is chewing on his bottom lip again, looking young, vulnerable, and downright charming as he waits for Dylan's answer, and Dylan can't bring himself to say no. He sits on the corner of his bed, sending the scythe tumbling to the floor, and nods curtly. "Talk."

Brendan shifts so he's facing Dylan, but he directs his gaze down to his lap. "I'm an idiot," he starts, and that definitely catches Dylan's attention. "I'm also shy." He looks up then and smiles slightly at Dylan's incredulous expression. "I know that's not the impression you got, because we didn't talk yesterday afternoon, I was drunk last night, and this morning things were oddly comfortable, but I am. I'm better here, because I know that most people get it, but back home...." His lips twist into a wry smile. "I'm sure you know how it is."

Dylan nods. He does know. He's never been even remotely shy, but he definitely understands the way mundanes react when he starts babbling on about something he thinks is *awesome,* and that they just don't understand at all. Incredulous stares were the best result he could hope for, and it was often worse. That doesn't exactly explain what happened at lunch, though.

"You were fine in the food court," he states flatly. "If Kelly and Sabrina had scared you, you would have run as soon as they jumped on me." Dylan would have understood that reaction. The girls could easily be overwhelming to someone who didn't know them, and though if Brendan had acted horribly he would have been offended on their behalves, he still would have understood where the reaction came from. This he didn't. "You didn't leave *then*, though, so why the hell did you run?"

"Because I'm an idiot, and I panicked." Brendan leans forward and looks Dylan in the eyes with an intensity that makes Dylan want to draw back some. "I can't imagine any of my friends just announcing I'm gay in a crowded room to someone I barely knew. I think I'd kill them." He twists his lips wryly, and his gaze loses some of its intensity. "When Sabrina said that, I felt like I was being put on the spot, I guess, and my body reacted before my brain did. By the time my brain caught up, it was too late to go back without looking and feeling like an even bigger idiot, so I just kept going."

It takes Dylan a moment to process the hidden meaning behind Brendan's words. When he does, his mouth drops open, and he gives Brendan a stunned look. "You ran when Sabrina said I was gay," he says slowly, still not quite believing what his brain is telling him, "because you're gay too?"

Brendan's head falls forward into his hands. What little of his face Dylan can see is flushed red, and the blush is creeping around the back of his neck to his ears. "Yeah."

"That's...." Dylan trails off, shaking his head. There really *aren't* any words.

"Stupid, I know." Brendan doesn't look up, and his hands muffle his words, but Dylan understands him well enough.

"That's one word for it," Dylan mutters. His shock is rapidly fading, and he's not sure if he's relieved or angry. Probably both. "I spent the last four hours worrying that I was rooming with a homophobic idiot, and I was going to be miserable all weekend, and you're *gay?*" He falls back on his bed with a moan, flinging his arms out dramatically.

Brendan hesitates a minute and then climbs off his bed and onto Dylan's. "I'm sorry," he says, looking down at Dylan apologetically. "I really wasn't thinking. I didn't mean to worry you." He sucks his bottom lip back into his mouth and wraps his arms around his knees. He's practically radiating worry and remorse.

It's giving Dylan a headache.

He's not ready to change out of his costume yet, though, so he doesn't rub at his forehead the way he wants to. He closes his eyes instead, fighting back the urge to groan. "I know," he says, because it's the best reassurance he can offer. It's *not* okay, but he can kind of understand. If Brendan isn't completely out of the closet, being put on the spot like that had to have been unnerving.

Brendan nods. "Thanks." Dylan expects him to get up then, but he doesn't. He sits right there on Dylan's bed, his arms wrapped around his knees as he gazes down at Dylan.

It's bothersome, and after another minute passes, Dylan arches an eyebrow. "Was there something else, or am I that irresistible?"

"Dressed like *that?*" Brendan barks out a laugh, throwing back his head and exposing the long lines of his tanned throat. "I don't think so," he continues once he's stopped chuckling.

"Hey!" Dylan pushes himself up on his elbows and gives Brendan his best mock glare. "This costume makes me extremely alluring."

Brendan lets his jaw drop and shakes his head. His eyes sparkle with mirth as they slide up and down Dylan's long frame and end up fixed on his face again. "Sorry. I prefer my men to be, well, *men*, not anthropomorphic personifications."

Dylan waggles his eyebrows. From the look on Brendan's face, he's sure it looks ridiculous with the skull makeup, but he goes with it anyway. The whole situation is ridiculous, so why not? "Oh, I'm *all* man under this, baby."

Brendan laughs so hard that he topples to the side, clutching at his stomach. "You did not just say that!" he manages between gasps for air. He starts to recover fairly quickly, but when he looks over, Dylan waggles his eyebrows again, and Brendan spends the next several minutes laughing so hard he can barely breathe.

By the time he stops, Dylan is seriously worried. "Are you okay?"

"I'm good." Brendan doesn't look at him though, just slowly stills until he's lying on his back, his chest heaving as he sucks in much-needed air.

Dylan watches carefully, his eyes focused on Brendan's chest. The top button of Brendan's already low-neck shirt has come undone, exposing even more of his tanned chest along with three freckles Dylan hadn't yet seen. He would really like to know if there are more still hidden by the soft cloth of Brendan's shirt, and now that he knows Brendan isn't going to crucify him for looking, he plans to take advantage of the situation.

He doesn't even realize how badly he's staring until Brendan pushes himself up on his elbows and looks at him with an incredulous expression. "Am I that irresistible?" he asks teasingly, the corners of his mouth curving up into a shy smile.

Dylan doesn't even think about his answer. "Yeah," he whispers, slowly lifting his eyes to Brendan's face. "You kind of are."

Brendan's shy smile blossoms into a full-fledged grin. There's a hint of blush on his cheeks, but he meets Dylan's gaze head-on. "You aren't so bad yourself when you aren't all covered in makeup."

Dylan has never been more torn about a costume in his life. He wants to wipe off all the makeup and let Brendan ogle as much as he wants, but he's also glad for the way it covers his flaming cheeks. This is not at all what he expected when Brendan asked to talk, and now that he's finally reading Brendan right, the whole weekend suddenly has the potential to be so much better than he'd dared to hope for. "Thanks," he mumbles, his eyes never leaving Brendan's body as the other man climbs from the bed.

"You're welcome." Brendan grabs his jacket and boots and pauses at the bathroom door. "Hey, Dylan?" he asks, suddenly looking and sounding uncertain again. "We're okay now, right?"

Even if Dylan wanted to say no, there's no way he possibly could. Brendan is halfway in the bathroom, peering around the doorframe with one hand clutching the molding. His eyes are wide and worried and looking especially bright, and his shirt is just askew enough to expose his collarbone. Dylan wants to lick it, to kiss his way up Brendan's throat and pay extra attention to the bottom lip that Brendan is again worrying, but it's too soon for that, so he just puts all of his amused affection into his smile as he nods. "Of course."

Brendan's answering smile makes Dylan's heart skip a beat, and as Brendan disappears into the bathroom, Dylan vows to do everything he can to make sure that soon they're more than just all right.

BRENDAN is sitting at Pulse, nursing a beer, when Tim and Matt find him. His guitar is on the floor in front of him, propped up on the wide end with the handle between his legs. It makes sitting a bit awkward, but he doesn't want to have to go back up to the room before meeting Kevin, and he's not about to just prop it against his chair and forget about it. That's asking for trouble.

Tim comes up behind him and slings an arm over his shoulder. "Brendan! Where have you been hiding?"

He twists and looks at Tim with wide eyes. "I've been here. Where we were supposed to meet an hour ago. Where have you been?"

"Costume contest." Matt rolls his eyes as Tim grins. It figures they were there.

Dylan had gone too and had invited Brendan along via text message, but he'd opted to go to the Brit Track's Are You Having a Laugh panel instead, jokingly claiming that he wasn't that gay. Dylan had texted back that he was, and Brendan had fought the desire to rush over to the ballroom just to see what he was missing.

"Oh? How was it?" he asks, giving Tim's outfit a once-over. "Did you pick up any costume pointers?"

"Matt did," Tim retorts. "I was just there to see what was cool." He leans forward, his eyes sparkling with excitement. "One group did this incredible costume from BioShock. Big Daddy and Little Sister. The drill arm *actually turned*. And a novice did this amazing Garthim costume."

Brendan turns to Matt with an amused grin. "He's really excited about this, isn't he?"

"It was pretty cool," Matt admits, only slightly grudgingly. "And the Crossed Swords didn't mangle anything too badly this year, either."

"No, but they showed us the exact same tricks *again* while we were waiting for the judging to finish." Dylan sets his drink— something pink and fruity that completely clashes with his Death costume—down next to Brendan and smiles around him at Tim and Matt. "I'm Dylan."

"So you're the roommate." Tim grins evilly as he takes Dylan's hand. "I'm Tim." His grin grows as he looks back and forth between Dylan and Brendan. "So I take it you two worked out your, ah, *issues*?"

"We talked," Brendan says shortly. He really doesn't want to go into this now, so he changes the subject and introduces his quieter friend. "Dylan, this is Matt, Tim's slightly better half. Matt, this is Dylan, my roommate."

Matt extends his hand and shakes Dylan's. "Nice to meet you."

"Likewise." Dylan returns the handshake, but as soon as they pull apart, his attention is back on Tim. "What issues did Brendan and I have to work out?"

"The ones that had him hiding in our room all afternoon." Tim leans across Brendan and lowers his voice conspiratorially. "Boy was all worried that he upset you and that he was going to have to crash with us for the weekend, which, believe me, he does not want to do." He puts his hands on his hips and strikes a flamboyant pose as he says the last few words. "It was cute how worried he was about having upset the hot roommate."

"He said I was hot?"

Tim lowers his voice even more, like somehow Brendan won't hear even though they're both leaning over him to talk. "Only about twenty times."

Dylan picks up his drink and slips around to slide an arm over Tim's shoulder. "Really? Do tell." He leads Tim off, leaving Brendan and Matt watching in stunned disbelief.

"Um, that's not going to be good, is it?"

Brendan shakes his head and slams back his drink. "I don't see how it could be."

DYLAN and Tim are still talking when Brendan has to go over to the Hyatt to meet Kevin for the open filk session. The conversation has apparently moved on from Brendan, but it's still with apprehension that he says good-bye, promising to meet up with Tim and Matt tomorrow and leaving Matt to join the conversation. Tim and Matt are good friends for people he only sees once a year, and he trusts them, but he really doesn't need them telling Dylan some of the things they know.

Not that it would matter, because he has no desire to be anything but a friendly acquaintance with Dylan, and it's not as though they'll ever see each other again after this weekend. It's not as though he wants to.

Really.

He keeps brooding on the issue as he takes out his guitar and begins tuning it, and his face has creased into an annoyed frown when Kevin sits down next to him, sliding up one eyebrow as he pulls out his own guitar. "Problems with the roommate still?"

"Yes. No." Brendan shakes his head. "Problems, yes, but not the problem I called you about. We worked that out."

Kevin's eyebrows creep higher as he situates his guitar on his lap. "So, then, what's the issue?"

Brendan looks around. People have seen the guitars and a few of them have stopped, waiting to decide if the performance is going to be something to make themselves comfortable for. If they don't start playing soon, they'll lose almost everyone waiting, but Brendan is in no hurry. Another crowd will form once they start playing, and Brendan doesn't play for the audience anyway. Kevin enjoys performing. Brendan just likes to play, and Dragon*Con is one of the few places he performs in public. Mostly he plays in the privacy of his own home, where no one but a few select friends and family can hear him.

"Tim and Matt are the problem," he says quietly, leaning down over his guitar to keep the curious from finding out what he's discussing. "I met them at Pulse after the Costume Contest, and Dylan found us. Now the three of them are conspiring."

"Conspiring? Really? Brendan."

"It's Tim and Matt." Brendan gives Kevin a pointed look. "Do you really think that they're going to pass up the opportunity to sabotage me?"

"Is there something to sabotage?"

"No."

"But?"

"Nothing!" When Kevin's steady gaze doesn't waver, Brendan ducks his head. "It's just, we're getting along again, and I know I'm not going to be in the room much this weekend, but it's nicer if we're being friendly. I don't need Tim and Matt scaring him away."

"Uh-huh."

Brendan narrows his eyes. "Don't give me that."

"Give you what?" Kevin looks and sounds far too innocent for Brendan's peace of mind.

"*That.*" Brendan narrows his eyes and glares at Kevin. "I heard that tone."

"What tone?"

"Whatever. Are we playing?" There's no point in arguing with Kevin right now. Brendan won't win, and he'll just end up even more irritated. He wants to calm down before going back to the room, not get riled up.

"Absolutely." Kevin pulls his guitar into his lap and strums a few chords, clearly expecting Brendan to just join in once he figures out what the song is. The smirk on his face is enough of a challenge that Brendan forgets about Kevin's teasing and just concentrates on the music, joining in after another few chords and opening his mouth right on time when the words start.

They've been playing for about half an hour to a steadily growing crowd when Kevin leans over between songs. "I don't think Tim and Matt scared away your boy."

"He's not my boy," Brendan murmurs without looking up. Kevin has been giving him songs in his ear like that for the whole set, and he's been only half paying attention to what Kevin has been saying. "Wait, what?"

Kevin laughs. "Sasquatch dressed as Death, right?"

"Yeah...."

"Over there." Kevin points with his chin as he begins strumming the opening chords to another song.

Brendan follows with his eyes and almost misses the opening words when his eyes fall on Dylan leaning against the wall, his arms crossed over his chest, hugging his scythe to his body. He looks away before Dylan can realize that he's staring, but he spends the entire song sneaking glances in his direction.

When the song ends, Kevin puts down his guitar. "Go. We'll catch up tomorrow."

"Go where?" Now it's Brendan's turn to act innocent, but he's far worse at it than Kevin, at least tonight.

Kevin just widens his eyes as he gives Brendan a pointed look. "I saw you trying not to watch him."

"I wasn't watching him. I just wanted to see what he thought."

"Uh-huh. Go ask." Kevin gives him that stern look that means he's not budging, and Brendan is forced to agree.

"Fine."

Brendan gathers his things, putting his guitar away slowly as Kevin starts his next song. He deliberately doesn't look at Dylan as he does so, but he keeps his eyes on the exit he's relatively sure Dylan will take if he leaves, and he's not sure how he feels when he finishes putting things away and Dylan still hasn't walked through it. Part of him really wishes that Dylan had left so he could put off the pending conversation a little longer, and part of him is glad Dylan waited.

He tries really hard not to think about what it might mean as he crosses behind Kevin and walks over to Dylan. "Hey."

Dylan grins, looking very macabre even with his skull makeup faded by the trials of the day. "Hi!" He sounds perky and his words are slurred a little, but his tone is affectionate, and Brendan can't really blame him for being tipsy. It's not as though he's completely sober himself. "You were great."

"Really?" Brendan rubs at the back of his neck with his free hand. "You think so?"

"Absolutely!" Dylan slings an arm around Brendan's shoulder and leans in close. "I love your singing voice."

His tone goes straight to Brendan's groin, and he swallows hard, glad for the guitar case in his hands and the long coat that goes down to his knees. "You do?" His tone is definitely *not* a squeak, but it *is* a little more high-pitched than usual.

"Oh yeah." Dylan's voice is hot against Brendan's ear, and suddenly the only thing on Brendan's mind is how he has to get out of here.

Now.

THERE'S a little voice in the back of Dylan's head telling him this is a very bad idea. It's been telling him that since he left Tim and Matt at Pulse and went to find Brendan, his head buzzing from the three drinks he'd downed as Tim and Matt had told him exactly what Brendan had said that afternoon and then had gone on to tell him exactly what they thought he should do about it. He'd scoffed at first, but the more he drank, the better of an idea it had seemed, and he'd found himself standing on the outskirts of the crowd around Brendan and his friend before he'd realized he'd even decided to go look.

Once Brendan had seen him, there was no way he could leave, but he had still told himself that he wasn't going to act on what Tim and Matt had suggested. They'd been drinking too, and Dylan had seen the look in Brendan's eyes as he'd left the three of them together. He'd been worried, and Dylan hadn't wanted to do anything to justify that, even though he really liked some of the things Tim and Matt were suggesting.

All his good intentions went out the window when he heard Brendan singing, however, and spending the trip back to the room with his arm slung around Brendan's shoulders isn't helping matters at all, especially since Brendan looks so very willing as Dylan turns, pressing him up against the just-closed door and leaning in close. "I'm going to kiss you now," he murmurs in a low voice that is only audible because of the silence in the room and his mouth's proximity to Brendan's ear. "Okay?"

Brendan nods and then tilts his chin up, meeting Dylan's eyes. "Yeah." He looks wanton and delicious, his eyes wide and surprisingly bright, and his freckles standing out against his skin.

Dylan doesn't ask again, he just leans in and presses his mouth to Brendan's, slipping his tongue inside when Brendan parts his lips. He tastes of beer and peanuts and something else that Dylan can't identify, but it's delicious, and as Dylan twines his tongue around Brendan's, he decides that it's something he would really like to taste again.

Brendan kisses back with fervor, wrapping his arms around Dylan's neck and deepening the kiss, slipping his tongue into Dylan's mouth as their lips move together. He slings his leg around Dylan's, pulling him closer with a suddenness that makes Dylan almost fall, but he catches himself, half on Brendan and half on the door, and they keep kissing.

It's not toe-curling or mind-bending or even remotely magical. It's sloppy and wet and Dylan's makeup is getting on Brendan's skin. The scythe and sword are crushed between them awkwardly, and Brendan's guitar has fallen to the floor and is leaning against their legs, threatening to fall between them if they move at all. It's still really nice, however, despite all that, and not just because they're both a little tipsy, although Dylan is sure that doesn't hurt.

Brendan tastes really good, and his body is warm and firm and fits wonderfully against Dylan's. His hands tangle in Dylan's hair like they were made for it, and their height difference is just enough that the kiss is perfectly angled. There aren't any fireworks or showers of faerie dust, but there are some sparks, and when Dylan pulls back, his chest heaving as he gasps for air, he can tell that Brendan felt them too. "That was—"

"Yeah." Brendan cuts him off with a grin. "Definitely. We should—"

Dylan doesn't give him the chance to finish.

SATURDAY

BRENDAN is already awake when his alarm goes off Saturday morning. He's pretty sure Dylan is too—he's heard him moving over the past half hour or so—but he immediately rolls over and grabs the phone anyway. If Dylan has somehow managed to fall back asleep, he doesn't want to wake him.

It ends up being a moot point.

Dylan is staring at him, his eyes wide and alert, though his expression and posture both say that he's really not completely awake. He smiles when Brendan glances at him, though, and Brendan's heart starts beating faster in his chest at the way Dylan's whole face lights up.

"Morning," he whispers, his own lips curling up into a wide, excited grin. Just looking at Dylan is making him feel giddy now, and if he hadn't already agreed to meet up with his friends for the parade—and they didn't already have a set of kick-ass coordinating costumes—he would skip it in favor of staying here all day. He and Dylan definitely have a lot of, ah, *talking* to do about what happened last night, and Brendan wants to get moving on it as quickly as possible.

"Good morning." Dylan sounds about as awake as Brendan feels. His voice is soft and hoarse, as though it's protesting being used so early. "You goin' to the parade?"

"Yep." Brendan's grin widens as he situates himself on his side so he can be comfortable while he watches Dylan. He tucks his left arm under the pillow, propping his head up some, and lets his right leg fall forward so he's half on his stomach. The three-foot gap between the beds is about all that's keeping him from wishing Dylan a proper good morning, but since he's not quite ready to crawl out from under the covers—even to make out—he'll settle for watching Dylan wake up. "You?

"Absolutely." Dylan flops over so he's lying flat on his stomach, one cheek smashed into his pillow and his arm dangling to the floor. "Marching in it."

Brendan shifts, already feeling restless and wanting a better view of Dylan. This is bound to be good. "As?"

"Sam Vimes." Dylan rubs at his eyes, blinking a few times before letting his hand fall back to the floor, his gaze following it. "I know it's unoriginal, using two characters from the same series this weekend, but Sabrina said she'd be Lady Sybil, and Kelly and Val said they'd be Cherry and Angua." He looks up, meeting Brendan's eyes with an expression that begs for understanding. "We've got a Carrot and Detrius too."

Brendan's grin grows as he gives in to his restlessness and sits up, pushes the covers back, and crosses his legs. "Captain Sam Vimes, Commander Sam Vimes, or His Grace, the Duke of Ankh, Commander Sir Samuel Vimes?"

Dylan looks flabbergasted as he pushes himself up, mimicking Brendan's cross-legged pose and staring at him across the gap between the beds. "Sir Sam," he says in an awed tone. "How did you...?"

"Just because I prefer Gaiman doesn't mean I'm ignorant about Pratchett. I told you I'd read a few of them. Besides, my sister, Mel? Total Watch Girl." He leans forward, his lips twisting up teasingly. "She would *love* you," he singsongs, grinning wider when Dylan blushes.

Dylan turns bright red as he rubs at the back of his neck, but when he meets Brendan's gaze, there's fire in his eyes. "Yeah, well, no disrespect to your sister," he says, crossing the gap between the beds and putting his hands on Brendan's shoulders, "I think I prefer her brother."

"Is that so?" Brendan tries to make the question a teasing one, but his voice hitches as he meets Dylan's smoldering gaze. Everything else he was going to say gets stuck in his throat as Dylan moves in, brushing his lips tentatively across Brendan's as though everything from the night before never happened.

Brendan freezes for a second, but as he feels Dylan about to pull back, he manages to make his limbs cooperate and he grabs Dylan's shoulders, holding him in place as he deepens the kiss. Dylan responds enthusiastically, and soon they're lying on Dylan's bed, making out like horny teenagers.

Dylan is an enthusiastic kisser, all over-eager hands and questing tongue, but once he finds a rhythm, he's good at it, and his fingers and tongue are almost magical with how quickly they get Brendan panting and gasping, his heart racing as most of his blood goes straight to his dick. He pushes his hips upward as he tangles his fingers in Dylan's hair, and they both moan as their groins brush together.

"Fuck, Brendan," Dylan mumbles, kissing his way up Brendan's jaw to his ear. "So hot."

Brendan can only make an incoherent sound as Dylan's hand slips under his pajama pants, wrapping around his cock and sliding down it with one smooth stroke. His hips jerk upward and he tips his head back, his eyes fluttering closed as he lets out a deep moan. Dylan takes advantage of his exposed throat, kissing along his pulse point and the underside of his chin as he continues to stroke Brendan's cock with rhythmic motions. When his thumb strokes across the tip of it, Brendan loses control completely, his hips jerking as he spurts sticky, wet fluid over Dylan's hand.

He's barely had time to register what happened when Dylan pulls his hand carefully out of Brendan's pajama bottoms and brings it up to his mouth. He makes sure Brendan is watching before he licks it, slowly dragging his tongue up his palm, twisting it so he catches every drop of Brendan's semen. His eyes never leave Brendan's as he slowly brings his tongue back into his mouth, and if Brendan hadn't just come, he probably would have again, just from the sheer hotness of it.

Instead, he surges upward, capturing Dylan's lips in a passionate kiss. The morning breath he'd tasted—and ignored—earlier is gone, replaced by a salty flavor that tastes far better on Dylan than it did on any other guy Brendan has ever tasted. He rolls them over as he slides his hand down Dylan's pants to return the favor. It doesn't take long before Dylan is gasping and moaning beneath him, his hips bucking upward, and when he lets out a particularly deep moan, Brendan grins and slides down, pushing Dylan's pajama pants out of the way and slowly licking along the length of Dylan's erection.

"God. *Brendan.*" Dylan's hands tangle in Brendan's hair, not tugging, just guiding as Brendan opens his throat and slowly slides Dylan's cock into his mouth. Brendan bottoms out and pulls back, one hand coming up to play with Dylan's balls as he sucks and licks, his lips sliding over Dylan's flesh. Dylan whimpers and moans, shifting and thrusting when Brendan slides his tongue over the tip and begging for more as Brendan's mouth works its magic.

It's not hard and fast like the hand job Dylan gave him. Instead, Brendan moves slowly, doing his best to draw out Dylan's pleasure as he moves, licking and sucking and blowing on Dylan's sensitive flesh. He slides his fingers from Dylan's balls to his thighs and back again, moving them in time with his mouth and grinning when Dylan starts making noises.

They're soft at first, so quiet that Brendan can hardly hear them over the beating of his own heart, but they grow in intensity until Brendan knows that the people in the rooms on either side of them have to know what's going on. He doesn't care, though, just keeps licking and sucking, pulling those glorious sounds from Dylan's mouth, and Brendan's gut starts to stir in response to them.

He shifts, sliding down on the bed for a different angle, pulls off Dylan's cock, and starts licking around the base of it instead. He can see it respond to the cool air of the room, stirring to both the blowing of the air conditioner and the soft ghosting of Brendan's breath, and he licks up each side before blowing gently across the tip. Dylan squirms, lifting his head and tightening his grip in Brendan's hair. "Brendan. Please."

Brendan grins and chuckles as he slowly licks up Dylan's cock one last time. He knows Dylan isn't going to last much longer, and he locks gazes with him as he opens his mouth and slowly takes Dylan's cock back in. This time, he moves faster, his tongue dancing over Dylan's skin as he moves up and down. His gaze never leaves Dylan's, and when his hands come up to play with Dylan's balls again, it's all that Dylan can handle.

"Gonna come," he manages, and Brendan just smiles and starts moving faster. His tongue slips over the tip of Dylan's cock again, and Dylan calls out Brendan's name, his hands clenching tightly in Brendan's hair as his body jerks and his seed spills down Brendan's throat.

Brendan swallows and licks Dylan's cock as he pulls back, making sure he gets every last drop. Dylan is sweeter than he expected, though probably he shouldn't be surprised given all the candy he's seen the man eat in the few hours that he's known him. That should be the real surprise, that he just gave a blow job to a guy he's known for less than forty-eight hours, but somehow, it's not. He feels like he should have known from the moment he met Dylan that they would end up here, like this, and more. It's not a feeling he's used to, but when he crawls back up Dylan's body and is immediately pulled down for a kiss, he decides that it's not one he's going to argue with.

Even if this is just for the weekend and he never sees Dylan again, it's going to be awesome.

DYLAN looks ridiculous. It's kind of the point—Sam Vimes's ducal outfit, even the Watch Commander version, *is* ridiculous—but he can't help but wish that he had something more attractive to wear. Once again, Brendan is outshining him, looking incredible in his outfit, while Dylan's costume, though amazing in terms of accuracy and quality, isn't exactly the most flattering thing he brought. It's only marginally better than his Death costume from yesterday, and he's starting to feel a little self-conscious about how he looks in his costumes every time he's near Brendan.

It's ridiculous, really, because everywhere else in the con, he knows that his costumes are incredible and he can look around and see how awesome everyone else thinks they are, but when he's alone with Brendan, he starts to worry about how *attractive* his costumes are. Unfortunately, he didn't pick his costumes for attractiveness. He picked them for how well they suited him, though realistically he probably would have made a better Carrot than Vimes. Sabrina had wanted a companion for her Lady Sybil, though, so Dylan is now dressed in velvet tights and feeling exceedingly awkward.

His only consolation is that Sabrina is going to look even more awkward than he does. She has a lavender dress that looks like a cross between a bad bridesmaid's dress and a medieval gown, a wig of blonde curls that makes Dylan's head itch just looking at it, and enough jewelry that Dylan is surprised that she can walk. Their other friends, in their ridiculous-looking fake armor breastplates, are going to look even more awkward.

Dylan is wearing his pirate costume all day tomorrow. Originally, he had planned to dress as Death again and then just change for the Pirate Party, but now he's feeling an intense desire to wear the one costume that makes him look really hot and will give him even the smallest chance of looking as incredible as Brendan does.

Okay, almost as incredible as Brendan does, because at this point, Dylan is pretty sure that Brendan looks incredible in *everything,* and there's no way that he can possibly match it. He would like to stop looking like the idiot dork when they're standing next to each other, though.

Frowning, Dylan puts the ducal coronet on his forehead and turns to strap on his sword. At least this time he gets to wear the cool weapon, though Brendan is wearing his dark suit and snakeskin boots with an air that very clearly says weapons are unnecessary. "You set?" he asks, slipping a pair of round wire-framed sunglasses onto his nose and grinning.

"Yeah." Dylan snatches his badge from the bed and follows Brendan out the door, checking to make sure he has his room key as well before pulling the door shut behind him.

Brendan heads straight for the elevator and Dylan follows. He debates trying to convince Brendan to take the stairs so they can avoid the usual elevator crowds and wait, but he hasn't managed to make up his mind by the time they reach the elevator bay, and since the elevator dings almost as soon as Brendan hits the button, it's rather a moot point anyway. Dylan isn't sure exactly how they managed to get an elevator so quickly, especially on the morning of the parade, but he's not going to argue with it. They're running late anyway, and if they can catch a break that will speed them up, he's not going to object.

Brendan leans against the glass wall as the doors close, and from the way he's tilting his head back and letting his shoulders slump a little, Dylan guesses that he's let his eyes slip closed behind his sunglasses as well. It's an amazingly sensual pose, his hands clasped on the bar behind his back and his throat exposed over the crisp collar of his button-down shirt and loosely knotted tie, and the elevator goes down three floors before Dylan manages to tear his eyes away and search for something else to focus on.

He doesn't find anything. It's an elevator, and since watching their descent out of the glass walls makes him feel vaguely ill, he's left with the shiny doors and the two panels of buttons, neither of which is capable of holding his interest for long.

Fortunately, they don't have to. No one else gets on, and the elevator coasts to a halt on the Atrium Level not long after they got on, the doors sliding open smoothly to reveal a large crowd waiting to take the elevator up to their destinations.

Brendan pushes himself from the wall with a groan, and Dylan shakes his head as he walks out behind him, his eyes firmly fixed on Brendan's ass. It's a nice ass, and the suit he's wearing is well cut and emphasizes it nicely, so Dylan doesn't see any reason to tear his eyes away. Brendan can hardly object after what they did this morning.

When they get out of the elevator bay, he takes a few quick steps and falls into pace next to Brendan. "So."

"Yes?" Brendan arches one eyebrow.

It looks especially fetching curving up over the sunglasses, and Dylan stares at it for a second. He's only jerked back to reality when he almost crashes into a Jedi. "Thought they were supposed to be aware of their surroundings."

"You should be too," Brendan mumbles as an amused grin spreads on his face. "You aren't distracted, are you?"

"What? No!" He's not, really. Okay, maybe a little, but that doesn't mean he's going to tell Brendan that, especially given why he's distracted.

"Uh-huh. Why didn't you see him, then? I think the big red lightsaber would have been a big clue he was coming, especially since he has it turned on."

"I—"

Brendan's other eyebrow slithers up to join the first. "Uh-huh."

"What?" Dylan spreads his arms wide in protest and narrowly misses hitting a girl in a faerie costume as she passes. "I didn't do anything!"

"But you want to?"

He has a point. Dylan *really* wants to shove Brendan up against the nearest flat surface and work on getting that suit off him. "No."

Brendan's eyebrows slide up further.

"Okay! Yes! I just…. Dammit, Brendan!" Dylan leans in close to Brendan's ear on the off chance that someone would overhear. "You can't go around looking like that and not expect me to want to do something about it!"

"As I recall," Brendan says with a grin, stepping just enough away from Dylan that they aren't pressed completely together, "you wanted to do something about it before I put the outfit on." He pauses. "And did," he adds with a fond grin.

"Yeah, but—"

Brendan just rolls his eyes. "Parade. Our friends are waiting for us."

"Yeah, yeah." He has a point, but that doesn't mean Dylan has to like it. "Who are your friends going to be dressed as, anyway?"

"Other *Good Omens* characters. We've got all four horsemen, my friend Peter is going to be Aziraphale, and Kevin and Laura are going to be Newton and Anathema." His face lights up as he talks, and by the time he's done, there's an extra spring in his step.

It's endearing.

"So you're not just marching alone, then."

Brendan throws a look at Dylan that clearly says he's a complete idiot for even asking the question. "Uh. Duh?"

"Well, you didn't mention your friends this morning."

"I didn't mention my *costume* this morning. Did you really think I was going to march alone, dressed like this? It's more of a group costume, don't you think?"

Dylan really hadn't, but now that Brendan mentions it, he's clearly right. Dylan had recognized the costume easily, but he's into

Good Omens and he knows that Brendan is as well, and the first thing he thought when Brendan had slipped on the snakeskin boots was Crowley, the rogue demon who works with the angel Aziraphale to stop the apocalypse. It honestly hadn't occurred to him until just now that not everyone will recognize it, even with the sunglasses, and that many people aren't going to be able to see the snakeskin on the boots anyway. Not from along the parade route.

"I guess." He shrugs. "I don't think many people are going to recognize the costumes even with that group, though."

"Doesn't matter. Someone will. And we know who we are, which is the most important thing."

Dylan just laughs. "And I know who you are too."

"Well, see? That just makes it all better."

"Doesn't it."

Brendan rolls his eyes and opens his mouth to respond, but instead he grins widely and hurries ahead, leaving Dylan to watch in amazement as he's hugged by a slender redhead in crimson biking leathers with a matching helmet tucked under one arm and a sword in her other hand. She looks incredibly hot and perfect to be War, and as Dylan watches, he realizes that it doesn't matter what the rest of the group looks like. Between Brendan and his friend, their group is going to get all *sorts* of appreciation.

BRENDAN motions Dylan over as he finishes greeting Elisa. She looks fabulous, perfect for the role of War, right down to the ruby studs spelling out *HELL'S ANGELS* across the back of her jacket. Brendan slides his hand over them as he admires the costume. They're genuinely poked through the leather, not attached some other way and just made to look like they are. "Shit, Lis!" he exclaims as Dylan walks up. "You ruined your jacket!"

She makes a sound of disbelief. "I have another one." Her eyes grow distant for a second and her grin grows. "A couple more, actually. This one was my least favorite and, fortuitously, worked best for the costume!" She preens a little, thrusting out her chest so Brendan can very clearly see the creamy swells of her breasts.

He rolls his eyes. He hates it when she acts up the role of ditzy girl and hates it even more when she does so while throwing around words like fortuitously. Unfortunately, Elisa knows it too and rarely passes up the opportunity to annoy him.

It's the sole disadvantage to having been friends with her since childhood, so he tolerates it, usually with good grace.

Today, he just ignores it, turning to Dylan with a wide smile. "Dylan, this is my old friend Elisa Cisneros. Lis, this is Dylan, my roommate."

"*Old* friend?" Elisa asks, lifting her sword slightly.

Brendan steps back, his hands held up in supplication, but Elisa just advances, her eyes narrowed though her lips keep trying to twist up into an amused grin.

Dylan steps between them before either of them can say anything more, grinning as he rakes his eyes up and down Elisa's body. "Nice costume."

She stops short, staring hard at him, her eyes narrowing even further as she meets his gaze. "*Really?*"

Brendan almost steps forward then—he knows that tone of voice, and it doesn't bode well for Dylan—but Dylan just grins wider and nods. "Absolutely. Best War costume I've ever seen. Not many people are willing and able to spend the money on a real crimson leather jacket."

Elisa's whole attitude changes just like that, and she perks up, practically preening again. "Thanks! I really like the idea of War being a woman, you know? And the description was just too perfect for me to pass up."

She has a point. It's almost as though Neil Gaiman and Terry Pratchett were thinking about Elisa when they wrote the description of War. The only thing she is naturally missing are the orange eyes, and she's taken care of that quite nicely with a pair of contacts. She truly looks the part, even more so than Brendan does in his perfect suit, snakeskin boots, and black sunglasses. Their group is going to be incredible in the parade.

"Well, you definitely pull it off," Dylan says, rubbing the back of his neck with one hand and adjusting his sword with the other. "You look great."

"Thanks! So do you." She frowns a little as she looks Dylan over more closely. "What's your costume again?"

"Sam Vimes, from *Discworld*. It's kind of ridiculous, but my friends wanted to do the Watch, so…." He trails off, shrugging, one hand still rubbing the back of his neck.

"I like it," Elisa says with a grin.

"Thanks." Dylan looks completely uncomfortable, but then his face brightens a little and he turns to Brendan. "I see Sabrina. I'll catch up with you later, yeah?" He doesn't even wait for Brendan to nod before he apologizes to Elisa and dashes off, heading toward a girl in a lavender dress who Brendan only recognizes as Sabrina because Dylan told him she was.

He doesn't have time to contemplate how a slender blonde suddenly turned into a slightly chubby brunette, though, because almost as soon as Dylan is gone, Brendan is jumped on, this time by Tim and Matt, who are both dressed in black biker gear with *HELL'S ANGELS* studded on the back. Matt is wearing a helmet with a dark, reflective visor so no one can see his eyes and a long black coat, while Tim has attached a fake black beard to his chin and is wearing a wig of short black hair that matches it. He's all in leather, from his boots to his shorter jacket, and the only issue with his costume at all is that he doesn't look gaunt enough to be starving.

Behind them is Robert, a friend of Tim's who Brendan has only met a few times, but who he has to admit looks fantastic in his dusty white leathers and his wig of long white stringy hair. He grins, the impish smile entirely at odds with his Pollution costume, and wiggles his fingers at Brendan and Elisa. "Hey."

Brendan nods in return as he's pounced on again from behind, this time by Peter Farces, another friend Brendan met at Dragon*Con and chats with occasionally on Twitter. He's wearing brown tweed pants, a cream-colored Oxford shirt, and a brown sweater vest. Wire-framed glasses with clear lenses are perched on his nose, and his light-brown hair is, per usual, a mess, though this time it's a *deliberate* mess. Brendan can't help but grin as he rakes his eyes up and down Peter's body, noting that Peter is doing the same to him.

"You look good," Peter finally says, grinning as he meets Brendan's eyes.

"You look like a librarian," Brendan returns, though there's no malice in the words. Peter is supposed to look like a librarian—Aziraphale is a used-bookstore owner—so it's really a compliment. Honest.

Peter just rolls his eyes and waves at Kevin and Laura, the last of their group to arrive. "We ready for this?"

Brendan has been ready since they decided to do this last year. He can't wait for the parade to start. "Absolutely. Let's go." He hooks one arm through Peter's and slings the other around Elisa's waist. This is going to be an amazing parade.

BRENDAN tries to find Dylan when the parade is over, but they weren't marching anywhere close to each other, and Elisa has attached herself firmly to his arm and doesn't seem at all inclined to let go, so after a few minutes of futile searching, he gives up and lets her steer him toward the food court, where she oh-so-graciously *lets* him treat her to lunch. They don't even try to find a table in the crowd, just head back to Elisa's room and sprawl across her bed, the food laid out on its wrappers in front of them.

"So your roommate seems nice," Elisa comments after a few minutes, her grin clearly showing that she thinks he seems much more than just "nice."

"He is. For the most part, anyway." Brendan shrugs. He's not going to tell her about what they did that morning if he can help it.

Of course, with Elisa, not talking is seldom an option. She's the kind of girl who lets you spill your guts to her the same way she lets you buy her things. Brendan never intends to do so, but when it's all said and done, he's left wondering what happened and somehow feeling as though it was all his idea. It's a good thing he only sees Elisa occasionally anymore. When they were younger, he was her favorite target to hone her skills on, and he's pretty sure that he's still her favorite target, if only because she finds it so easy with him. He really has to make it harder for her.

If only.

"For the most part?" she asks, her perfectly thinned eyebrows elegantly arched toward her hairline. "What do you mean *for the most part*, Brendan? He's not…?"

She trails off, but Brendan knows exactly what she means. She was there in high school when he came out to a few people he shouldn't have, and she was the one who helped him keep it together through the few weeks that were left in the school year. She's the only one who knows the full extent of his reasons behind not being completely out and proud, and Brendan knows that there's only concern behind her words.

"No." He can't help but laugh a little as he shakes his head. "Dylan's gay too. One of his friends outed him to me rather unexpectedly at lunch, and I think he thought I was homophobic for a while. We talked it out, though," he finishes hurriedly before Elisa can comment. "It's fine."

"But why would he think that?" She tilts her head curiously to the side, her long hair sliding over the red leather of her jacket as she moves.

"I ran?" Brendan rubs at the back of his neck. He really doesn't want to go through this again, but if he doesn't tell Elisa, someone else will, and that will be worse for him, he's sure of it. She'll be completely supportive, but she'll also be a little offended that he didn't feel he could tell her, and rightly so. She's the one person he can tell anything to.

Well, just about anything. The jury is still out on if she gets to know what he has going on with Dylan.

Probably, he'll tell her once he figures it out for himself. They haven't exactly talked about it, after all. It could be just a convention fling, which would be fine with Brendan. He didn't come here looking for true love or happily ever after, after all. They'll talk if and when they feel they need to. Until then, Brendan is going to enjoy himself and do his best to keep whatever it is between them as private as he can. Elisa will ask questions he's not sure he wants to think about right now. They might well be moot points anyway.

Elisa smacks his arm. "Brendan! What did you do that for?"

"I panicked!" Brendan takes a long sip of his drink, hoping that Elisa will let it go, but when she doesn't, he sighs and settles the cup back between his crossed legs. "I know, all right! Tim and Matt and Kevin already yelled at me yesterday. And Dylan and I talked. We're fine, I promise."

"You sure?" She straightens her head a little as she stares hard at him, her lips pursed and her expression stern. When he stares back, she relents a little, slumping slightly as her expression softens. "I just worry about you, Brendan," she says, putting one carefully manicured hand on his arm.

The red of her nails stands out against his dark jacket, and he stares at her fingers for a moment before looking up at her with a satisfied smile. "Very sure."

"*Brendan!*" Elisa laughs as she pulls her hand back. "Are you implying what I think you're implying? You sly dog!"

"We didn't—"

"Sleep together?"

"Yeah." It's a futile distinction at this point in time, but he has to make the effort.

Elisa isn't buying it. "So what *did* you do?"

"I'm not kissing and telling!"

"But you did kiss, right? *Please* tell me you kissed!" When he hesitates, she leans in, squeezing his arm tightly. "Come on, Brendan, you owe me."

"For what?"

"Do you really want me to get into that?"

He probably doesn't. Elisa has a crazy-long memory, and she'll probably dredge up some favor she did for him when they were eight that she'll swear he never paid her back for, and he'll have no way to prove otherwise, despite the fact that he knows he's done her at least as many favors as she's done him. "Not really."

"Well, then." She beams widely. "So tell. Come on. I really want to imagine the two of you kissing."

"It's probably not as great as you imagined." Halfway through the sentence realizes what he's doing, but it's too late then, so he just gives in and keeps talking. It's easier in the long run. "We were both drunk and still wearing our costumes."

"Which were?" Elisa's eyes are alight and she keeps leaning closer and closer, clearly hanging on every word. "Come on! I need the full picture!"

"Well, I was wearing my Tristran outfit and he was, uh, Death. From *Discworld*."

Her nose wrinkles. *"Death,* Death? Like, seven-foot-tall skeleton that wears a long black robe and speaks in small caps? That Death?"

"Yep."

"But he's a skeleton!"

"Yep!"

"Was it a mask?"

"Nope." Brendan's grin keeps growing with each of Elisa's questions. This is actually a lot of fun, and he's kind of sad that she's going to figure it out soon.

"Not a mask?"

"Nope."

"Then... makeup?"

"Yep."

"But... he's a skeleton!"

"Yep."

"Brendan. You kissed him while he had his face painted like a skeleton?"

"Yep." He's grinning widely now. Elisa's expression is completely comical, especially since Brendan found the experience to be more than a little enjoyable—though he did wish there had been a way to avoid smearing the makeup all over his face as well—and she seems to think that it was horrific. "Well, actually," he corrects, his lips twitching as he tries to hold in a laugh, "he kissed me. And then I kissed him back."

"Still!"

She shudders dramatically, and Brendan can't hold in his laughter any longer. He falls backward on the bed, his whole body shaking, and it's only Elisa's quick reflexes that keep his drink from spilling all over the bed. "You know I wasn't actually looking at him while we kissed, right? I closed my eyes."

"But didn't the makeup smear?"

There's really no denying that. No matter what happens in the movies, when real people wear makeup like that all day long, it smears, especially when they start making out. "Yeah. So?"

"But—"

"It was worth it, Elisa." He pushes himself up on his elbows and grins widely at her. "*Definitely* worth it."

"Really?"

"Oh yeah." Brendan's smile grows as he thinks back to how the morning started. He would put up with a lot more than just some easily removable makeup smeared over his face the night before for that kind of wake-up call.

Elisa leans in close, her grin spreading. "Do tell."

DYLAN doesn't find Brendan again until after dinner. He goes back to the room after the parade, hoping to catch him, but he's not there, and before he works up the courage to call or text, Sabrina comes and drags him off to the food court and the Dealers Room. They meet up with Kelly and Valerie, one of the other girls who walked in the parade with them, for lunch, and while they reminisce about the parade and the things they've seen so far at the convention, Dylan forgets all about calling or texting Brendan.

He doesn't remember at all until he's back in the room, pulling up his bank balance on his laptop to make sure he really can afford to buy everything he really wants to get when he goes back to the Dealers Room. He can, assuming he doesn't find anything really expensive that he has to have when he goes to visit the Art Show, but there's still the question of whether or not he should. There are lots of shiny things he really wants to buy, but he's not sure how many of them will ever do anything more than sit on a shelf once he gets them home, and if he's perfectly honest with himself, he has to admit that he really is running out of shelf space that he can devote to knickknacks.

Okay, he's actually running out of shelf space period, but he can justify buying more shelving units for something that he actually gets use out of, like books or DVDs. Of course, if he has to buy another shelf for books or DVDs, then he'll be able to justify buying more meaningless knickknacks, but he can't just buy the shelves for the shiny things he wants to get from the Dragon*Con merchants. That would somehow be crossing a line that he's not quite ready to cross.

It's kind of a ridiculous thought, and when he automatically turns to share it, he remembers that he hasn't actually seen Brendan since just before the parade, and he suddenly misses him. It's a strange feeling. When he'd set up the roommate arrangement, he'd counted on most of the days being like today, where they don't see each other at all except briefly in the morning and at night, but with everything that's happened in the past forty-eight hours, he finds that he really wishes Brendan were around.

It's a completely unexpected feeling and one Dylan isn't sure how to handle. He doesn't want to just blurt it out, and he definitely doesn't want to do anything to make Brendan suspicious or drive him away, but he really wants to explore whatever they have between them and see where it goes. Maybe it won't be anything, and maybe it'll just be them having fun at Dragon*Con, and they'll never see each other again afterward, but maybe it'll be something more than that. Now he just has to decide how he's going to figure it out.

He's holding his phone, contemplating whether or not he should call or text Brendan, when the door to the room opens and Brendan walks in. He looks just as good as he did this morning, though his pants are a little rumpled and his sunglasses are tucked into the pocket of his jacket. The tie is also a little looser than it was when he started out, but as far as Dylan is concerned, that just makes it easier to get it off, which Dylan *definitely* wants to do.

"Hey!" he says as he drops his phone on the desk, hoping that he doesn't sound too thrilled to see Brendan. He wants to ask where Brendan has been, and what he's been up to, and if he wants Dylan-shaped company next time, but he figures that would completely scare Brendan away. "You have a good afternoon?"

"Mostly?" Brendan flops back on his bed, his arms out at his sides and his feet dangling off the edge. "I tried to find you after the parade, but Elisa kidnapped me and made me buy her lunch and tell her all about you."

Dylan has to fight to hide the thrill he feels when Brendan says he looked for him. "All about me?" he asks, hoping he sounds nonchalant, despite the excitement and sudden apprehension that are at war in his gut.

"Yeah." Brendan pushes himself up on his elbows and looks sheepishly at Dylan. "I, uh, maybe let it slip that we kissed last night, and then she made me tell her the rest."

"Made you?" Dylan clears his throat. That was *way* too close to a nervous squeak for his manly pride. "What do you mean *made you*?"

It still comes out sounding a bit too high-pitched, but Brendan thankfully just widens his eyes and shakes his head. "Exactly what it sounds like. Are you okay?"

Dylan clears his throat again. "I'm fine," he says hurriedly. "Just, uh, ahem, got a frog in my throat. How did she make you?" he presses, anxious to keep the conversation away from his sudden inability to speak in a normal tone of voice.

"Uh-huh." Brendan doesn't look like he believes him, but he shakes his head and flops back down on the bed without further argument.

He also doesn't answer Dylan's question, and Dylan finds himself forced to ask it again. "So, uh," he manages in a mostly normal voice, "how did Elisa *make* you tell her about me? And what exactly did you tell her, anyway?" His voice is squeaking again by the time he finishes, but he doesn't care anymore. He really wants to know the answer. If he can convince Brendan to share what he told Elisa, he might know what kind of chance he has to even see where this goes.

Okay, so based on what happened this morning, he's pretty sure he has a decent chance, but there's always that off chance that Brendan immediately regretted it. It's not like they talked about it, after all.

Brendan pushes himself back up, but he doesn't exactly look at Dylan. His eyes dart all over the room until he lets his head flop back so he's staring directly up at the ceiling, his neck stretched out above his exposed collarbone and distracting Dylan. "Not much. I mean, I told her that we kissed. And that it was worth getting your makeup smeared all over my face. And I, um." He pushes himself up into a sitting position and leans forward, meeting Dylan's eyes with a terrified gaze. "I told her what happened this morning too."

Dylan isn't sure how to respond to that. On one hand, it's good that Brendan is talking about what happened with his friends. It means he's not trying to hide this, and that means that Dylan maybe doesn't need to worry so much. On the other hand, it's not good that Brendan is talking about what happened with his friends. Dylan rather wanted to keep it between the two of them, at least until he knows what it might mean for him, and it's not like he actually knows Elisa. Clearly, she's one of Brendan's good friends, but Dylan has only talked to her for maybe five minutes, and all he really knows is that she's at least somewhat familiar with *Discworld*, and that she likes *Good Omens*. They're both commendable qualities as far as Dylan is concerned, but that doesn't mean he's going to be best friends with her.

"You did?" This time he's not even embarrassed that it comes out sounding more like a squeak than anything else. He is definitely concerned about Elisa knowing, and if squeaking gets that point across to Brendan, then Dylan is fine with doing so. "Why?"

"Look." Brendan rubs the back of his neck as he leans forward further, his expression a strange mix of sheepish and earnest. "The thing about Elisa is that she has this way of making you do things, only it doesn't feel like she's making you at the time, you know? Like, I bought her lunch today, and I had decided that I wasn't going to buy her lunch, because I *always* end up buying her lunch, but then we were standing in line and somehow I ended up paying for both of us and feeling like it was my idea!" He shakes his head as he jumps to his feet and starts pacing back and forth in front of the mirror. His hand comes up to pinch the bridge of his nose, and suddenly he starts to resemble a stressed-out CEO more than the demon from *Good Omens*.

Dylan can't stand to watch it. He jumps up and positions himself so that Brendan has to walk right into him on his next pace across the room. When he gets close, he's still not looking up, so Dylan grabs his shoulders before he runs into anything and steers him to the bed. "Calm down."

"I'm trying. I just—" Brendan takes a deep breath as he looks up at Dylan. "Sorry. I've been friends with Elisa since I was five, and I love the girl, but she can drive me crazy sometimes. I miss her when I'm at home, but every time we get together, I'm reminded how much better it is that she lives in Los Angeles now, and we only see each other a few times a year."

Dylan isn't sure what to say to that, so he sits down next to Brendan with his hands clasped in his lap so he won't do anything that he might regret later, like pull Brendan down for a passionate make-out session. This clearly isn't the time for that, even though Dylan's brain seems to have set up on a single track and won't let go of the idea that Brendan looks eminently kissable in that outfit, even when flustered. "I'm sorry?" he finally ventures once the silence gets to be too much, and he has to say or do something or he'll go nuts.

"Don't be." Brendan laughs bitterly as he sags forward, resting his head in his hands. His shoulders are slumped, and Dylan has to fight back the urge to pull him into his arms and comfort him. "I'm the one who told Elisa."

"Yeah, well, it's not that big of a deal. I mean, so long as you didn't say I was horrible or anything like that, I think we'll be okay."

Brendan turns his head to look at Dylan, his lips twitching as he fights back a grin. "I told her you sucked and that it was the worst hand job I've ever gotten in my entire life," he says, deadpan. His eyes are sparkling, though, and when his lips twitch again and then curl up into a full-blown smile, Dylan relaxes, the weight that had landed on his chest with Brendan's words lifting as suddenly as it had arrived.

"Well, there's no way I can match *you.* You've had *years* of practice jerking yourself off. That was my first try."

For a moment, Dylan isn't sure that Brendan understood what he was trying to imply and he starts to think that maybe he should avoid jokes like that, particularly if he wants to have the chance to improve his performance, but then Brendan's shoulders start shaking, and before Dylan can really process what's happening, he breaks out into wild laughter, clutching at his stomach and slumping so far forward over his knees that Dylan is afraid that he's going to fall to the floor.

It's not far to fall, and it's not as though Brendan could possibly hurt himself, but Dylan doesn't care. It's an excuse to put his hands on Brendan, and he moves without really thinking, grabbing him around the waist and leaning back, until they're both sprawled out on the bed, Brendan halfway on top of Dylan.

When he finally manages to stop laughing, Brendan rolls off, sits up, and looks down at Dylan with a raised eyebrow. "You that anxious to improve on what you did this morning?"

He most definitely is, but he also doesn't want to seem too eager, so he slides his hands behind his head and grins up at Brendan. "Only if you want me to. I wouldn't want to leave you feeling inferior by beating you on my second try, after all."

"Brat." Brendan smacks him in the stomach, lightly enough that it's clear he's only playing, but hard enough that Dylan feels it through the layers of fabric that make up his costume.

"Ow! Jerk!" Dylan smacks back, hitting Brendan lightly on the arm, and then suddenly, they're rolling on the bed, laughing and wrestling and calling each other ridiculous names. It's several minutes before they break apart, both gasping for breath as they lie on their backs, staring up at the ceiling.

After a minute of silence, Brendan rolls onto his side and waggles his eyebrows at Dylan. "So. Was it good for you?"

"You're going to have to do more than that if you want to impress me, baby."

Brendan's grin broadens. "If you insist."

It turns out Brendan's suit really does look better on the floor than it does on Brendan.

DYLAN stands on his tiptoes as he scans the crowd in the Capitol Ballroom. He's looked for Brendan at every party he's been able to get into without any luck, and he's starting to think that maybe Brendan changed his mind—or worse, lied—about going to a party tonight. They didn't exactly talk much after exchanging blow jobs, and while it hadn't felt like Brendan was fleeing when he'd left to go meet Elisa at the Fun with Demonology panel, now Dylan is starting to wonder if he had been, especially since he's not answering his phone either.

The Capitol Ballroom is quieter than Dylan had expected, but it's still loud and crowded, and it takes Dylan a while to scan all the tables. It's hard to see everyone clearly, and he almost misses Brendan slouched in a chair against the wall, his arms crossed over his chest and his sunglasses pushed all the way up on his nose. He's alone, and he doesn't look very happy, so it's with trepidation that Dylan crosses the room and stops in front of him.

"Hey," he says quietly, shuffling from foot to foot and wishing that his Sam Vimes costume had pockets he could shove his hands into. He feels odd with them hanging free, and he's pretty sure he's fidgeted more at this convention than he has in the past month. At the moment, he's flexing his fingers, trying to resist the urge to twist them together as he waits for Brendan's response.

He needn't have worried.

Brendan's entire face lights up when he looks up and sees Dylan. "Hi!" he exclaims, smiling widely and tucking his sunglasses into his pocket. His eyes sparkle as they meet Dylan's. "You found me!"

Something relaxes in Dylan at those words, and he matches Brendan's grin with one of his own, though he adds a quirked eyebrow to the look. "Yep. Took a while, though. I was starting to think you didn't want to be found."

"What? Why?" Brendan's brow furrows. "I told you where I was going to be."

Dylan sits down next to Brendan, angling his body in the chair so he's still mostly facing the other man. "You said a party, not which one, and you weren't answering your phone, so…." He trails off, shrugging. Brendan can fill in the end of the sentence himself.

"You called?" Frowning, Brendan slides his hand inside his suit jacket and pulls out his phone. "Really?"

"Yep. Texted too. Several times."

"Huh." Brendan's frown deepens as he hits buttons. "I didn't hear it ring. I'm sorry."

He looks so worried that Dylan immediately forgives him. "It's all right. The signals are kind of crap down here, anyway."

"Tell me about it." A look of relief flashes across Brendan's face before he rolls his eyes. "You can have a full set of bars, take two steps, and have none. It's crazy."

"Yeah." Dylan slouches back in his chair. After a minute of companionable silence, he looks around, frowning slightly. "So this party…."

"I'm not sure *party* is the right word." Brendan rolls his eyes again. "Peter told me I should come, but it's not what I expected. I don't think it's what he expected, either, to be honest, but he's having more fun than I am." He leans in close to Dylan and lowers his voice. "You wanna head upstairs? I hear the Kingdom of Loathing party has free alcohol."

Dylan doesn't know who Peter is, and he only has a vague idea about what Kingdom of Loathing is, but free alcohol sounds wonderful and overrides any other objections he might have. He likes the idea of Kingdom of Loathing—a parody of the more popular Massively Multiplayer Online Role Playing Games with a deliberately simple interface and stick-figure graphics—and combining something that clever with alcohol at Dragon*Con can only lead to a good time. "Hell yes." He stands and gestures for Brendan to precede him. "Lead on."

Brendan leads the way up the stairs and around the corner. The Party of Loathing is in one of the regular track rooms, with someone stationed at the door to check IDs, and Dylan has a moment of panic before he remembers that he tucked his driver's license in with his money and pulls it free for the door guard to inspect.

Inside, music is pounding loudly. They navigate past the chairs piled to either side of the door, stepping around the Kingdom of Loathing banner spread out on the floor in front of some of the chairs, and head straight for the table with the drinks. Brendan pours himself something yellow while Dylan takes something orange, downing it quickly and refilling his glass before stepping away from the table.

"Thirsty?" Brendan asks as he follows.

Dylan just nods. This is more what he imagined a party would be like, but now that he's here, he's not sure what to do. The music is too loud for any real conversation, and most of the guests at this point seem to be people who actually play the game. There are even a few in costumes that come straight from it—dressed all in white with black tape or paint used to create the stick-figure look. He feels a little out of place, which is odd for him, especially at Dragon*Con. He's used to occasionally feeling out of place in the real world, but the con is one place he can always feel like he fits in, and this sensation of not belonging isn't sitting right.

"So," he says after a minute, grabbing a chocolate and berry treat from the table and sitting down on one of the nearby chairs. Chocolate always makes sense, and it's probably safer in the end for him to be sitting near it than near the drinks. At least this way if he overindulges he won't regret it in the morning. He might regret it in a few years when he has to buy all new clothes and redo all his costumes because he's gained too much weight, but at least chocolate won't lead to him making any stupid decisions or worshiping the porcelain god.

"So," Brendan echoes, sitting next to him. He watches Dylan expectantly, and when Dylan doesn't say anything, he snags two chocolate concoctions from the table and hands one of them to Dylan.

"Thanks." Dylan's fingers brush against Brendan's as he takes the candy, sending a sudden physical jolt through his body that reminds him exactly why he was nervous when he first went looking for Brendan tonight, and he immediately downs the rest of his alcohol to forget about it.

It doesn't work, and before Brendan can say anything, he crosses the room with swift steps and pours them both another glass.

It's definitely a drinking night.

Brendan is waiting with a curious expression when Dylan returns. He takes both cups carefully from Dylan's hands, setting them on the floor under his chair, where they'll hopefully be safe from wandering feet and waving arms, and pulls Dylan back down into his chair with a gentle tug on his forearm. "What's wrong?"

He looks entirely too serious for a Saturday night party at Dragon*Con, but Dylan doesn't know what to say to make it go away, so he just shrugs. "Nothing." Nothing that he's willing to tell Brendan about just yet anyway, blow jobs and invitations to parties aside. He doesn't even know if he wants to say anything, much less how or when. Even if he did, this is definitely not the time or place. "I promise," he adds with what he hopes is a convincing grin.

Brendan doesn't look like he buys it, but he doesn't press the issue, either, just shrugs and pulls the alcohol out from under the chair. "If you're sure."

"I am."

"Okay," Brendan agrees after what feels like forever. He hands Dylan his glass before tipping the other one up to his lips, drinking it all in one go before heading back to the drinks table and filling his glass again.

Apparently, Dylan isn't the only one dealing with issues the wrong way tonight.

BRENDAN leans heavily on Dylan as they stagger back from the Sheraton to the Marriott. Fortunately, it's only a block and a half, because he can definitely feel the way the earth is spinning tonight, and he's pretty sure it's picked up a bit of a wobble as well.

Still, as long as it doesn't wobble too much, he's kind of glad for it, because it's giving him a great excuse to wrap his arms around Dylan's waist, something he's wanted to do all day long but hadn't dared to until he'd drunk enough to give him the courage. Exchanging blow jobs in their shared hotel room is one thing, leaning on each other in public is something completely different, and Brendan doesn't know how Dylan would react to it if they weren't both just a little tipsy, and the earth wasn't conspiring to make it near impossible for either of them to stand up straight.

It's a little weird, because most of the other people who are passing between hotels don't seem to have any trouble staying upright on their own, but Dylan is leaning just as heavily on Brendan as Brendan is on Dylan, and Dylan's arm is slung over Brendan's shoulder, so he knows it's not just him. Maybe it's not a conspiracy. Maybe the earth is on Brendan's side and wants to give him a reason to act on his wishes.

If that's the case—and it's looking more and more like it is with each person that passes them—then it would be wrong not to act on it. Clearly, Mother Nature, or God, or someone with phenomenal cosmic powers is on Brendan's side, and he wouldn't want to risk upsetting them. They could make his life a living hell. He *has* to listen.

They make it all the way inside the Marriott without falling over or letting go of each other, but when they get to the escalator to go up to the Atrium Level, they have to step apart. The escalator is only wide enough to ride single file, and even though Brendan keeps his fingers fisted in Dylan's doublet as he lets the other man go in front of him, it's not the same. He misses the connection he felt when they were wrapped around each other.

Dylan starts to follow the line to the next escalator, where they'll have to ride up the exact same way, so Brendan tightens his grip, angles toward the elevator bay, and yanks, pulling Dylan out of the line. He stumbles, but Brendan catches him, and even though the earth doesn't seem to be shaking them together anymore, Dylan's clumsiness is another perfect excuse for them to walk wrapped around each other.

Brendan takes it.

When they reach the elevator bay, it's amazingly empty, though at this point, Brendan wouldn't care if it were packed full of people. All he cares about at the moment is the wall space, and there's usually plenty of that no matter how packed the elevator bay is, as most people want to wait as close to the elevator doors as possible so they have a better chance of cramming into the crowded car. At the moment, Brendan just wants a wall he can push Dylan up against.

He hits the call button with one hand as he presses Dylan up against the wall next to it, angling up on his toes and sliding his hands around Dylan's back as he moves. Their bodies are pressed close together, and when Dylan's hands slide around his back, Brendan leans up and kisses him.

It's sloppy and wet, and they've barely started when the elevator bay starts filling up, but Brendan doesn't mind at all. Dylan's lips are warm and soft, and he tastes like fruit and chocolate, and even though Brendan is usually shy, right now kissing Dylan in front of all the people who are filing into the elevator bay seems like the best idea he's ever had. Dylan seems to agree and kisses back enthusiastically, making noises that go straight to Brendan's groin and wriggling just enough that Brendan can feel his hard cock pressing through the thin material of his tights and doublet.

The elevator can't come fast enough.

When it dings and opens, Brendan moves faster than he should be capable of, given the amount of alcohol he's consumed, and jerks Dylan inside, quickly pressing the button for the eleventh floor as he shoves Dylan up against the railing that goes around the glass walls. They're packed in, pressed tightly together, and Brendan quickly discards the fleeting thought he'd had about behaving on the ride up and starts kissing Dylan again.

He's going to regret this in the morning, he's sure, but right now he can't care at all.

Sometimes, alcohol is a wonderful thing.

The elevator has emptied some by the time it reaches the eleventh floor, but Brendan doesn't pull back from Dylan at all until the doors open to let them out. Even then, he keeps Dylan as close as possible, which isn't hard at all, as Dylan seems to be in complete agreement about how they desperately need to stay wrapped around each other, and he slings his arm back around Brendan's shoulder as they exit the elevator and stumble toward their room.

Dylan presses him into the door as he fumbles with the keycard, and they practically fall inside when the door finally pops open. Brendan catches himself on the wall, Dylan catches himself on Brendan, and it's nothing short of a miracle that neither of them tumbles to the floor and hits their head on the dresser or the wall.

Somehow—Brendan never does figure it out, though he thinks it involves Dylan grabbing him around the waist and doing this complicated turning, twisting thing with his body—they end up tangled together on Brendan's bed, their arms and legs wrapped around each other in a way that boggles Brendan's mind. Of course, his mind is pretty easy to boggle at the moment. He's just sober enough to admit that, so that might not be saying much.

Or it could be saying everything.

They untangle quickly and surprisingly easily, and just as quickly, Brendan rolls over onto Dylan, pinning him to the bed and kissing him again. He still tastes like fruit and chocolate, and Brendan can't get enough of it. He slips his tongue into Dylan's mouth, sliding it along Dylan's tongue as they explore each other's mouths and bodies, their hands roaming as their tongues delve and taste and tease.

Brendan loses himself in the sensation, his world narrowing to Dylan and the way they're moving together. Dylan rolls them over, pinning Brendan to the bed and sliding his hands under the suit jacket. Earlier, when Dylan had proved so adept at divesting him of the suit, Brendan had worried about it getting wrinkled and had managed a momentary protest when Dylan had started to slide it from his body piece by piece. Now, he knows how good Dylan is at removing it, and though he's definitely going to need to make sure it isn't ripped—it's a pretty expensive suit, after all—he doesn't care one iota about wrinkles. That's what dry cleaning is for, and if he really wants to wear the costume again before the convention ends, the hotel will be happy to clean and press it for him if he'll only pay them an outrageous fee.

He wriggles around, pawing at Dylan's clothes even as Dylan deftly frees him from the jacket and tie and undoes the buttons on his shirt. He manages to free Dylan from his doublet before Dylan slides down, running his hands along Brendan's thighs before grabbing the boots and pulling them off. It lacks the teasing finesse of earlier, but it gets the job done and, more importantly, frees up Brendan's feet so that Dylan can pull off his pants and boxers. He does so with one swift movement, leaving Brendan only in the unbuttoned white shirt, which he lets slide off his shoulders as he surges up to meet Dylan's lips.

They don't break apart for some time, even as they wriggle around, pulling Dylan's clothes off as well and tossing them to join Brendan's on the floor. When they're both fully naked, Brendan pulls back, resting his forehead against Dylan's and grinning widely, his shoulders heaving as he fights to control his breathing. "So," he whispers, his smile growing as he speaks, "how are we…?"

Dylan's answering smile is blinding. "You. In me."

Brendan can *definitely* live with that. "Yeah." He kisses Dylan one more time before rolling off and staggering into the bathroom. He hears Dylan calling after him, confused, but he's not gone long enough to worry about answering as the lube and condoms are tucked right where they're easy to find in the outer pocket of his toiletries kit. He grabs both and holds them up in answer to Dylan's question as he climbs back onto the bed.

"Oh." Dylan's grin grows until it's almost impossibly wide. "Awesome."

It definitely is. Brendan slides his way up Dylan's body until he's laid out flat on top of him, their cocks rubbing together as he presses his lips to Dylan's pulse point and kisses his way down his neck to his collarbone. Dylan moans, tilting his head back and giving Brendan better access as he keeps kissing Dylan's skin, slowly making his way across Dylan's throat and up to his ear. He sucks the lobe into his mouth as he slides his hand between their bodies, wrapping it around Dylan's cock and stroking firmly.

Dylan's hips thrust up into Brendan's hand, and his head tilts back even further as he scrapes his thankfully blunt nails down Brendan's spine, making a sound that goes straight to Brendan's groin. He wriggles and thrusts, and suddenly lying on top of Dylan with their cocks brushing is both too much and not enough. He has to move, now, or he's going to shoot off like an overexcited teenager and completely ruin the evening.

"Gotta," he mumbles as he wiggles around, grabbing the lube and pouring too much of it onto his hand before slipping down to kneel between Dylan's legs. The slick liquid drips off his fingers onto the comforter, leaving wet spots on the fluffy white cover, but Brendan doesn't care. Housekeeping will get it in the morning or after they check out, and since he fully intends to make several more stains over the course of the weekend, it really doesn't matter which.

The lube drips across Dylan's skin, round drops falling on his stomach and thighs as Brendan slides his hand between Dylan's legs and slips his finger into Dylan's hole, pressing slowly inside. Dylan is tight around his finger, but he used enough lube that it still slides in easily, the muscles giving just enough to let him push his digit all the way in. Dylan tenses, hissing and clenching his fingers in the comforter, but when Brendan stops moving, wanting to give him time to adjust, Dylan grabs Brendan's shoulder with one hand and yanks him down. "Don't."

"Okay," Brendan breathes, curling his finger inside Dylan as he's pulled in for a kiss. Dylan moans into his mouth, and he twists the finger again, making Dylan jump and gasp and start begging for more.

Brendan inserts another finger, and then another, stretching Dylan as quickly as he can. They're both hard and hot, their cocks leaking pre-come, and Brendan doesn't dare touch Dylan anywhere as he stretches him open, because if he does, it will be over before it really begins.

Finally, after minutes that feel like eternity, Dylan shifts. "Enough," he growls, again grabbing Brendan's free arm and pulling him down so their torsos are touching and their cocks are brushing together. Brendan slides his fingers out, wiping them on the comforter as he fumbles around with his other hand, looking for the lube and condom, but Dylan grabs them both, ripping open the foil packet and holding it out questioningly. "Can I...?"

"No." Brendan takes it with shaking fingers and rolls it on with care. He desperately *wants* Dylan to do it, but he's going to come just thinking about it, and tonight there's no way he's going to last at all if he lets Dylan touch him, so he takes the lube from Dylan's slack fingers and pours it over his cock, using far too much and just letting it run off so he doesn't have to stroke himself. "Ready?"

Dylan looks up, meeting Brendan's eyes with a shameless stare, and hooks his legs around Brendan's waist. "Yeah."

Brendan thrusts forward, moving quickly and trusting that he prepared Dylan enough. He can't take this slow, not tonight, not with Dylan looking so wanton beneath him and the alcohol running through his body lowering his inhibitions and his stamina. He freezes when he bottoms out, trembling as he waits for Dylan to let him know that it's okay to move. It seems to take forever, but just when the pressure around Brendan's dick has become almost unbearable and he thinks he's going to come without moving at all, Dylan nods.

He's tight and warm and feels amazing as Brendan thrusts, pulling almost all the way out before pushing forward again, changing the angle slightly as he moves. It feels incredible and Brendan moans deeply, joining his voice to Dylan's in cries of pleasure. He's leaning over too far to do anything other than thrust without toppling onto Dylan and ruining the moment, but Dylan slips one of his hands between their bodies and starts stroking himself in time with Brendan's increasingly frantic thrusts. The look on his face is one of complete pleasure, want, and need, his eyes rolled back in his head and his mouth open just slightly as he gasps and moans in reaction to Brendan's movement.

It's not long before he comes, his mouth opening wider and his body shaking and clenching around Brendan as his seed spills out, spreading onto both their bellies. He calls out Brendan's name in a choked voice, his free hand clenching in the comforter beneath them as his eyes flutter closed.

It's enough to send Brendan over the edge. He collapses forward as his body trembles, his seed shooting out as Dylan clenches around him. It's fast and messy, and he collapses in a boneless heap on top of Dylan as soon as he's finished, his muscles now lacking the strength to support him.

They lay together for several minutes before Brendan finally pulls out, rolling off Dylan and discarding the condom in the bathroom trash. He grabs a washcloth from the sink and wets it before stumbling back into the room to find Dylan lying on the other bed, the covers thrown back and his tanned, naked body contrasting beautifully with the crisp white sheets.

Brendan freezes between the beds, unsure which one he should collapse onto, but when he holds out the cloth to Dylan, Dylan catches his wrist instead and tugs him down on top of him. Brendan falls with a grunt, and for a moment they're all tangled together uncomfortably, elbows and knees in all the wrong places, but then they get straightened out with Brendan stretched out next to Dylan, looking over at him with a silly grin. "Hi."

"Hey." Dylan takes the washcloth and wipes them both off before throwing it onto the other bed. "We should definitely request housekeeping change the bedding tomorrow."

"Hmm." Brendan isn't so sure they should—he definitely wants to do this again and there are only so many times he's willing to call housekeeping for fresh bedding in a weekend—but he's too tired to argue. Instead, he lays his head on Dylan's shoulder and lets his eyes close. He lets out a contented sigh as Dylan pulls the covers over both of them and falls asleep with a smile on his face, feeling more relaxed than he has since he arrived.

SUNDAY

DYLAN wakes up slowly. He's wrapped in a cocoon of comfort and warmth, and he doesn't really want to climb out of it, but the pressure on his bladder keeps building, and he's eventually forced to move and take care of the problem. Without opening his eyes, he carefully disentangles himself from Brendan and stumbles from the bed, his eyes remaining closed for a few steps, until he stubs his toe on something they'd dropped on the floor the night before and he's forced to crack them open enough to navigate to the bathroom without harming himself further.

When he returns to the bed, he pauses, frowning down at the way Brendan is sprawled across the spot Dylan had been lying in, as though he'd tried to follow Dylan when he got up and had run out of energy after just reaching his arm over. He's curled into a vague question-mark shape, his back still pressed up against the pillows that weren't pushed to the floor in the middle of the night, his head lying in the spot Dylan's chest had previously occupied, and his right arm stretched across the rest of the bed with his fingers curled at the edge of the mattress. It's cute, especially the way Brendan has buried his face in his arm as though he's trying to block out some nonexistent light, but it's also problematic. There's no way Dylan is getting back into bed without waking Brendan, and he's not sure he's ready to do that just yet. He remembers everything they did the night before, remembers what he was thinking—or not thinking, as the case really was—at the party, and he's still not ready to have the conversation that led to him drinking so much.

He's afraid that if he wakes Brendan, he'll have no choice but to have it.

On the other hand, he's also not willing to climb into the other bed. They are definitely going to have to let housekeeping in today—he can see the spots on the comforter from here—and next time they do this, they're going to have to be sure to pull back the covers first. It will be far less embarrassing to have the sheets covered with jizz when housekeeping arrives than the comforter. It looks like they were so anxious last night that they were acting like horny teenagers who couldn't hold back at all.

Okay, they actually *were* acting like horny teenagers who couldn't hold back at all, but that isn't the point. The point is that no one else needs to know that, and leaving jizz on the comforter and making the bed basically useless until housekeeping arrives is not the way to maintain secrecy.

Now, if only they had managed to think about that last night, this morning would be a lot simpler.

Of course, they didn't, which is why Dylan has to try to slide into bed and back under Brendan without waking him up. It's a delicate process, but Brendan apparently responds far better in his sleep than Dylan does, and soon Dylan manages to coax Brendan onto his back, leaving just enough room so that he can slide into the bed and pull the covers back up over them both. He only makes it as far as sliding back in before Brendan rolls back over, resting his head on Dylan's chest and flinging his arm across his waist as he makes a contented sound.

It's cute, but inconvenient, and Dylan is left with no choice. He gently strokes a finger down Brendan's cheek. "Brendan."

"Hmmm?" Brendan's nose twitches as he blinks his eyes open and peers blearily at Dylan through his lashes.

"Scoot over. I'm falling off the bed." He nudges Brendan lightly, urging him to move toward the center of the bed.

Brendan scrunches his nose and scoots until his back is against the pillows again. He lets his head fall on the pillow he was supposedly sleeping on, but he holds up his arm in invitation and doesn't lower it until Dylan has scooted over as well and he can tuck it back across Dylan's waist. "Better?" he asks sleepily, moving his head to rest it on Dylan's chest once more and letting his eyes close.

"Much." Dylan smiles fondly as Brendan snuggles in closer, shifting and squirming until he's practically on top of Dylan and then letting every muscle of his body relax simultaneously. It's as though Dylan is covered with a thick, heavy, breathing blanket, and he wouldn't change it for anything.

"Good." The word is muffled against Dylan's chest. "Now go back to sleep. 'M still tired."

Dylan laughs. "All right," he says, pressing a kiss to the top of Brendan's head. "Sleep well."

Brendan mumbles something in response, but Dylan doesn't understand it, and he doesn't ask Brendan to repeat it, either. It can't be that important; Brendan is already mostly asleep, and it's doubtful that he'll remember the conversation when they wake up later.

Still grinning, Dylan lets his eyes slide closed and wraps his arms around Brendan, holding him close as they both slip back into slumber.

IT FEELS like Brendan has just fallen asleep again when he's awakened by a pounding on the door. He jerks, every muscle in his body tensing at the noise, and springs from fast asleep to wide awake instantly. Dylan is somehow still asleep, so Brendan carefully climbs off the bed and stumbles to the door, cautiously navigating around the discarded clothing that they hadn't bothered to clean up last night and snatching a pair of boxers from the floor as he passes them.

Dylan is still naked and completely exposed, but the bed isn't visible from the doorway, so Brendan just concentrates on stepping into the boxers as he moves across the room. Based on how they fit, he's pretty sure they're Dylan's, but it's too dark to tell for sure and it doesn't matter anyway. He's not planning to keep them on once he takes care of whoever is at the door.

The pounding comes again before he gets there, and this time it's accompanied by a muffled yell. "Housekeeping!"

"Just a minute!" he says, casting a glance over his shoulder to make sure that they haven't woken Dylan. He's stirring, but he still appears to be asleep, so Brendan hurries his steps as he nears the door and leans heavily on the doorframe as he pulls it open.

The hallway is bright, and even up here on the eleventh floor he can still hear some of the noise wafting up from the Atrium Level. He squints as he peers at the short dark-haired woman in front of him. "Yeah?"

"Sorry," she says, assuming an apologetic expression as she takes in his sleep-rumpled state and the darkness behind him. "I'll come back later."

Brendan manages a smile. In his opinion, it's far too early to be up, particularly on a Sunday morning after the night that he had, but clearly, many con-goers are, and he can hardly fault the woman for doing her job. "Thanks."

It's a lot harder to stumble back to bed than it was to get to the door. The adrenaline that had coursed through his system at the first noise has faded, leaving him drained from the rush and still exhausted from the events of last night. Brendan almost falls over when he tries to take the boxers off, and he's sure the bouncing of the bed had to wake Dylan, but when he crawls back in and settles next to him, Dylan still seems to be sound asleep.

It's perfect, and Brendan lays his head back on Dylan's shoulder, closes his eyes, and relaxes. He's half asleep by the time he's settled, and he fully expects to drift off within seconds.

He doesn't.

Instead, he spends several minutes lying perfectly still, his eyes closed and his breathing deliberately slow, waiting for sleep to overtake him. He's exhausted, tired down to his bones, and so worn out that it *hurts*, and yet he can't sleep. His mind is racing, mostly thinking about how wonderful it would be if he could just drift off, but he can't, and soon he feels like he's being mocked by the red numbers on the clock.

It's only nine in the morning, not too early to still be sleeping given how late he was up yesterday and especially not too early given how exhausted he is, but he's awake now, and somehow his body doesn't want to fall back asleep.

He's debating whether or not he should get up and try to see if one of his friends is awake when Dylan stirs under him. Brendan immediately tenses, worried that somehow his restlessness woke Dylan, and he frowns as he slowly lifts his head. "Did I wake you?"

"Sorta." Dylan slides his hand up Brendan's back and pushes his head back down. "Don't worry about it. Go back to sleep."

"Can't." Brendan shifts around until he's slightly more comfortable, but now his eyes don't even want to stay closed. He's definitely awake for the near future, despite the weariness and exhaustion that's seeping through his bones.

"Why not?" Dylan lifts his head and peers down at Brendan. "You look exhausted."

"I am." Brendan sighs, his whole body deflating further so he's lying over Dylan like a limp noodle. "I think I'm too tired or something." He manages a half-hearted shrug as he tips his head up to look at Dylan.

"Too tired?" Dylan widens his eyes and quirks his lips in amusement. "Are you sure you're just not tired enough?"

"Uh, yeah?" That's a stupid question. If that were the case, every muscle in his body wouldn't feel as though it's trying to hold extra weight every time he moves. "Doesn't matter, anyway. It's not like there's anything I can do either way." He's not getting up yet. He's comfortable even though he can't sleep, and unless Dylan makes him move, he has no intention of doing so anytime soon. Even if he can't sleep, he can at least rest.

"Maybe not," Dylan agrees with a shrug, "but there's something *I* can do." He waggles his eyebrows as he slides his hand over Brendan's hip, slipping it between them and wrapping it around his cock.

Brendan gasps as he thrusts his hips forward. He's already growing hard, and when Dylan starts stroking, his body responds with enthusiasm and energy he didn't know he possessed. It's not long before his toes are curling and his fingers are clenching, and when Dylan leans down and captures Brendan's lips in a gentle kiss, it's all over. Brendan comes, hard, moaning into Dylan's mouth as his body trembles.

Dylan fumbles on the floor and grabs the boxers Brendan just stepped out of, using them to wipe them both off before kissing Brendan again. They're dry, so they're not ideal, but they work well enough, and when Dylan tosses them back to the ground, Brendan makes a contented sound and cuddles closer. Dylan was right; he could easily fall asleep now, but first he slides his hand down Dylan's chest, intending to repay the favor.

He's stopped by Dylan's hand over his before he reaches Dylan's belly button. "Don't," Dylan whispers before kissing his forehead, "I'm good."

It seems wrong to just drift off without doing *something* for Dylan, but when Dylan wraps Brendan's hand in his and positions them over his heart, Brendan gives in. He'll make it up to Dylan later, with interest. For now, he's going back to sleep.

DYLAN wakes to moist warmth sliding down his cock. He shifts and moans, and when he opens his eyes, he sees Brendan between his legs, his lips parted as his tongue flicks out to lick the tip of Dylan's erection. The sheets are still up to his shoulders, and he looks positively sinful, his lips moist and red, his hazel eyes sparkling, and his freckles standing out across the bridge of his nose.

He grins widely and winks before opening his mouth and taking Dylan all the way in, slipping his lips down to the base of Dylan's cock without hesitation and slowly pulling back, hollowing his cheeks and sucking as he moves.

It feels *marvelous,* and it takes every bit of Dylan's willpower not to buck his hips up as Brendan swirls his tongue over the tip once more before sliding his mouth back down. He's doing wonderful things with his tongue and lips, and when he slides his hand up Dylan's thigh and starts rolling his balls between his fingers, Dylan gives up any pretense of control.

His eyes flutter closed as he tips his head back, a deep, loud moan escaping his throat. He slides his hands up Brendan's shoulders and tangles them in his hair, holding and guiding him, though he manages to maintain enough presence of mind to let Brendan choose the pace. It's the best blow job Dylan can remember having, and that includes the ones he exchanged with Brendan already. It's more intimate somehow, more meaningful, and Dylan isn't sure if it's because now they've had sex, and this is more than just a precursor to it, or if it's because Dylan has decided that he wants to see where this can go after the convention, if he ever gets up the nerve to talk to Brendan about it, or something else entirely.

Regardless of why or how, Dylan is brought to the edge quickly, as though he's a fumbling teenager and this is the first blow job he's ever gotten, and it's with great effort that he holds back and tugs at Brendan's hair. "Stop," he gasps as he tries to squirm away from Brendan's sinful lips. This isn't what he wants this morning, but if he doesn't get Brendan to stop, he's not going to be able to do what he really wants.

The look on Brendan's face when he pulls back is so hurt that the first thing Dylan does is tug at his shoulders, guiding him up until he can kiss the worry off his face. "I want you inside me when I come," he whispers, his forehead pressed against Brendan's as he looks straight into worried hazel eyes. "Wasn't gonna last."

"Oh." Brendan blinks, his eyes unfocused for a second, and then his lips curve up into a wide grin, and he kisses Dylan hard. "Oh!" he repeats when he pulls back, his hand already fumbling around on the nightstand for the lube and condoms that were left there last night. At the time, it had seemed that Brendan was being optimistic grabbing a strip of the foil-wrapped packets, but now Dylan is glad he did, because it means that neither of them have to get up to fetch more.

Dylan takes the condoms from him, setting them on the pillow next to him, and waits as Brendan coats his hand before taking the lube as well. He understands why Brendan had to do that part himself last night, but this morning, Dylan wants the pleasure, wants Brendan to be as hard and as close as he is right now when they join, and he's not going to take no for an answer.

He doesn't even have to ask. Brendan stretches him quickly, taking advantage of the fact that he's still loose from last night, and sits back on his knees, his hands behind him to hold him up and his cock curving up proudly from between his legs. Dylan grabs the supplies as he sits up, ripping the packet open with his teeth as he moves and pulling Brendan in for a brief kiss before rolling the condom down his cock and pouring the lube into his hand.

Dylan kisses Brendan again as he spreads the lube over the condom with steady strokes. His tongue dips into Brendan's mouth as his thumb flicks over the tip of his cock, and Brendan moans deeply, his hips thrusting forward into Dylan's hand. "Dylan... come *on*," he whimpers, pulling back just enough to speak. "Need you."

He's practically incoherent, which is just how Dylan wants him. He kisses Brendan again and lies back on the bed, shoving a pillow under his hips and bending his knees. Brendan doesn't wait, just leans forward and pushes right in, his body braced above Dylan's as he thrusts. He slides one hand between their bodies, wrapping it around Dylan's cock, and strokes it in time with his thrusts, short quick strokes that leave Dylan pushing his hips upward, desperate for more.

They move together, their strokes and thrusts finding the perfect rhythm. It's magical; at least it would be if something that leaves him sticky and sweaty and completely limp with pleased exhaustion can be called *magic*. Whatever it is, though, it's perfect, and when he comes, screaming Brendan's name, he doesn't even care how thin the hotel room walls might be or who else could possibly hear him. It feels too good for him to care, and when Brendan does the same just a few seconds later, his eyes rolling back in his head as his body shakes, and Dylan's name spills from his lips, it's the most perfect moment Dylan has ever had at Dragon*Con.

Brendan collapses on top of him, breathing hard, and peers up at him with heavy eyes and a soft smile. "Best Dragon*Con *ever*," he whispers, and Dylan has to agree.

BRENDAN grins widely as he and Dylan walk into the Dealers Room. It's packed, just as he expected, and it's mostly the same vendors who have been here every year since he started coming, but it's still one of the best things about Dragon*Con. Even with the room so stuffed full of people that it's almost impossible to move down some of the aisles, it's fun, and navigating through the crowds without losing whoever he's shopping with is part of the experience for Brendan. It's not going to be quite as hard this year—Dylan is taller than any of Brendan's other friends—but it won't be without its challenges. Plenty of people will be in costumes that make them taller, and the crowd is so thick that even if he can see Dylan, he won't necessarily be able to get to him.

He's looking forward to it.

They hold up their badges as they follow the crowd through the door and head to Aisle A, where they'd decided to start while eating lunch with Kelly and Sabrina. The only way to get through the room and make sure they find everything they might want to see is to move systematically, and Aisle A is the easiest to start with, even with everyone crowding around the T-shirt table at the beginning.

Brendan is honestly surprised that the girls aren't with them—Dylan had invited them at lunch—but apparently, they both had panels they weren't willing to miss. There are panels Brendan wants to go to today as well, but he had decided while getting ready that morning that he's willing to skip them all to spend the afternoon strolling around the Dealers Room, Exhibit Hall, and Art Show with Dylan. He'll worry about getting to the panels if they finish with time for him to get to any of them. If not, well, the only thing he's really excited about today is the Pirate Party, and that's not until late. Even if they stay until the rooms close, he'll still have plenty of time to meet his friends for dinner, change, and get to the party.

They move slowly, keeping pace with the crowd, and Brendan lets his mind wander. The first aisle is all stores he's seen year after year, most of which don't interest him at all, and he's content to just stroll through it on his way to the more interesting stuff, but when he starts to pick up the pace, Dylan grabs his elbow and yanks him into the small leather booth on the left.

"Slow down!" he hisses, letting go of Brendan's arm to run his fingers over the leather goods. "I want to shop!"

"All right!" Brendan holds his hands up in surrender. He hadn't been going all that quickly, but even after only three days he's already figured out that subtlety and patience are not among Dylan's strengths. It's kind of endearing, actually, though he suspects that it also means his arm will be rather sore before the day is out.

Dylan just narrows his eyes and glares for a minute before picking up key chains and book covers, running his fingers over the leatherwork before looking at the prices. "You're not one of those people who want to rush through and only stop at specific booths, are you?" he asks, his tone suddenly wary. "Because I like to browse."

"Only after I've been through a few times," Brendan replies easily, fingering one of the key chains. It's nice work, and the design is something his brother would probably like, but Brendan isn't buying anything yet. Besides, he's years past the time when a little trinket was all he gave Alex for Christmas, and he no longer brings back small gifts for all his family and friends every time he takes a trip. He may come back later—there's no reason not to buy it, either, if it's still calling to him after he's looked at everything—but he's going to complete at least one circuit of the booths before he makes any decisions.

Dylan finishes a minute after Brendan slides the key fob back on the hook, and they continue on their way, meandering through the room at the pace of the crowd. They don't say much—it's too loud for real conversation—just point out items of interest and drag each other into various booths so they can give items a closer look.

It's a little more physical than Brendan is used to—his friends usually just yell for him to stop if he gets separated, while Dylan has the tendency to tug on whatever body part of Brendan's is closest—but it's fun. Shopping with Dylan is an experience Brendan isn't likely to forget anytime soon, and it's making the Dealers Room far more interesting than he had expected it to be.

About midway through, they reach the booth Brendan has been hoping they'd find. He stands a little to the side, Dylan pressed close behind him to stay out of the way of the crowd, and watches with an indulgent smile on his face as a petite blonde argues with a customer. The man is the kind who seems to think that he's doing the vendor a huge favor by even looking at the stuff that's displayed, and by the time he leaves with a promise to think about coming back, the woman's face is twisted in annoyance.

Brendan steps easily into the vacated spot. "Problems, Tara?"

"Brendan!" Tara's face lights up and she waves her hand dismissively. "Nothing I can't handle." Her nose wrinkles briefly and she leans forward, resting her hands on the table. "So how are you? I didn't think I was going see you this year when you didn't stop by with stuff for me!"

"Yeah. Well." Brendan rubs at the back of his neck. "I had to fly this year, so I didn't have room to bring much of it in my luggage. Sorry. I just have my tools and a little bit of wire."

"Fly?" Tara's brow furrows. "Why?"

"Nate is an ass."

Tara laughs long and hard. When she manages to stop, she arches an eyebrow and crosses her arms over her chest. "Seriously, Brendan. Why'd you fly?"

"Because Nate is an ass," he repeats. "He bailed on me last minute, so I had to find a roommate and book a flight."

"*Find* a roommate? *You?*"

Her disbelief is evident in her voice, but her words remind Brendan that Dylan is hovering nearby and he reaches over and tugs him closer. "Yes. Me." He flashes a quick grin at Dylan before returning his attention to Tara. "This is Dylan Rojers, my roommate. Dylan, this is Tara Reglan, a friend."

Dylan extends his hand, his dimples flashing under his pirate hat. "Nice to meet you."

"You too," Tara replies, her expression awed as she shakes Dylan's hand. As soon as she lets go, she rivets her attention on Brendan again. "You're *hanging out with him*? What the hell has gotten into you, Brendan?"

Brendan flushes as his mind goes to all the other things he's done besides *hang out* with Dylan the past few days. At least he's topped both times so far, so he doesn't have to bite back the urge to tell her that Dylan's gotten into him. Still, he has been uncharacteristically friendly, and Tara would never believe what they've done, not that he has any intention of telling her. She's a friend, but not a close one, and it's definitely none of her business. "Shut up."

Dylan laughs and slings an arm over Brendan's shoulders. "So what is Brendan usually like?" he asks, leaning in and winking conspiratorially at Tara.

"Shy," Tara replies without hesitation. "I don't think he would have talked to me at all when we first met if he hadn't admired a bit of the metalwork on some of my jewelry. Even then, Nate did most of the talking, and Nate doesn't even *know* anything about metalwork!"

"And Brendan does?"

"Uh, *yeah*. He hasn't showed you his stuff?"

"No. He hasn't." Dylan's tone makes it clear that is going to change at the first opportunity.

Brendan immediately starts plotting how to distract him. It shouldn't be difficult, and it could be very pleasant for both of them.

Tara leans across the table and lightly smacks his arm. "Brendan! Why not?"

"I *do* have other interests, you know," he shoots back, jerking his arm away from her hand. "And I'm not as shy as you seem to think I am."

"You were pretty shy when you met me."

"That was *six years* ago. And you're pretty intimidating!"

"Me?" Tara looks Brendan up and down before glancing at her own body. She's several inches shorter than Brendan, and though she's wearing a kick-ass outfit of high-heeled boots, tight black pants, and a tightly laced black-leather corset over a white peasant blouse, she doesn't exactly look scary. "You're kidding, right? I sell *jewelry*."

"Awesome jewelry," Brendan counters. "And you're gorgeous."

"You're gay."

"So?" Brendan rolls his eyes. "Just because I'm not attracted to you doesn't mean I can't appreciate your beauty aesthetically."

"Really? That's the best you can do?" Tara rolls her eyes and turns to Dylan. "Help me out here. *Please.*"

"Um." Dylan's eyes widen and he swallows hard as Tara directs her full attention at him. "I think he can, actually."

"Oh, whatever." Tara makes a dismissive gesture. "I still maintain that you're shy, Brendan."

"I didn't say I wasn't shy, just that I'm not as socially inept as you seem to think I am." At least, he isn't anymore. The less said about his younger years, the better.

"Maybe not *now*," she replies with surprising insight, her lips curling as her eyes flicker over to Dylan. "Back then you were. You could hardly talk!"

"I was overawed by your stunning work."

Tara snorts. "Of course you were. 'Cause, you know, your work *sucks*. That's why I sell it."

"You sell his stuff?" Dylan peers down at the table with increased curiosity. "Is any of this his?"

"Sadly, no. He didn't give me any of his stuff to sell like he has in the past." Tara narrows her eyes at Brendan again. "I could have used it too. I had a couple people ask."

"I told you! It wouldn't fit in my bag!" Brendan holds up his hands in surrender. He'd take a step back, but the aisle behind him is teeming with people, and there's no room to move if he wants to stay in front of Tara's table. "It's not like she sells all that much of it anyway," he adds as an aside to Dylan.

"Only everything he gives me."

Dylan holds up his hands, mimicking Brendan. "Would you two like me to step away so you can talk to each other?"

"No!" they exclaim simultaneously, both directing glares at Dylan.

"Sorry!" He lowers his hands and his eyes, tucking his thumbs into his wide belt. "Carry on."

"His stuff is fantastic," Tara tells Dylan, completely ignoring Brendan. "You really should make him show it to you." She turns back to Brendan. "Please tell me you at least brought enough that you can show him."

"Yes," Brendan says with a sigh. "I have a few pieces with my tools."

"Good!" Tara beams. "Be sure you show it to Dylan."

"I will," Brendan promises. "*Later*. Now, however, we have to go." He grabs Dylan's forearm in an iron grip and grins at Tara. "Help the people who actually want to buy something."

"You'll buy something."

"We'll see!" he calls back over his shoulder, flashing a grin as he drags Dylan away. Truthfully, he probably will buy something, if only just to support Tara, but he can't let her think that he's a sure thing. It's so much more fun to wait until the last minute and let her think that he's not going to buy than to just buy straight off, especially since Tara is good at getting worked up.

It's one of Brendan's chief sources of amusement in slow times, though he's careful to never let it go too far. Tara can be temperamental, after all, and he doesn't want to really hurt her feelings, just tease her.

They're around the next aisle when Dylan looks over at Brendan and grins. "So. When do I get to gush over your work?"

Brendan groans. "Later." *Much* later.

THE Art Show isn't as crowded as the Dealers Room and Exhibit Hall were, but there are still a fair number of people inside. It's a different atmosphere, though, quieter and more respectful, though it's still difficult to get up close to some of the tables on the outside.

The room is laid out in sort of a twisting spiral pattern, a little difficult to follow, but they meander through slowly, taking their time to stop and look at various pieces of art. Some of it is amazing and some of it just isn't Dylan's thing, but they at least stop at every booth, glancing over the wares, if nothing else. There are some incredible pictures that Dylan would love to have on his walls along with a few that he's sure his mother and sister would love as well, despite not being all that into fantasy art. The pictures are just so incredibly gorgeous that he can't imagine anyone not liking them.

Brendan hovers by the big Celtic art display for some time, looking at the various pieces with his hands clasped behind his back. It's a very Tristran pose, and it looks almost as though he stepped right out of the movie—or book, as Dylan is sure he'd insist. The costume looks as good as it did on Friday, though now Dylan is even more determined to get him out of it. Brendan's Crowley suit looked *awesome* on the floor, but Dylan is sure that Tristran's coat will look even better.

Not that he's at all biased or anxious to find out.

"See something you like?" he asks, slinging an arm over Brendan's shoulder again. The Celtic stuff is nice, a little different from a lot of the other items in the show, but nothing that Dylan would buy. He can see its appeal to other people, though, and why it's popular. It's just not for him.

"Eh." Brendan shrugs. "My mom likes Celtic things; I thought maybe I'd get something for her. Dunno, though." He grins and slides his arm around Dylan's waist, slipping his fingers under Dylan's belt as he starts walking again.

Dylan comes without protest, a wide grin on his face. He could get used to walking around like this.

They get a few amused looks, but for the most part, everyone ignores them until they get to the booth Dylan almost forgot was going to be here. Jonathon Hutchins doesn't make it every year, and some years when he comes, he sets up in the Dealers Room or doesn't bring his wares at all, but this year he's brought his smaller, more artistic pieces and is exhibiting them in the Art Show. A few of the more ornate designs are set up for bidding, and all but one of them has been bid on at this point, but he also has plenty of smaller items—bracelets, necklaces, and bracers, mostly—out just for display or sale. He's taking the money for them right at the booth, with no need to go up to the cashier, and Dylan finds himself fingering a leather bracelet without even thinking about it. Jon taught him most of what he knows, and his leatherwork will never be as good as Jon's is, though he'd like to think that he's fairly good at it by now.

Not good enough that he'd ever think about exhibiting in the Art Show at Dragon*Con, though.

"Dylan!" Jon greets him, grinning widely and patting him on his free shoulder enthusiastically. "How are you? And who's your friend?" He puts a special emphasis on the last word that leaves no doubt he's already aware that Dylan is more than just friends with Brendan.

Too bad Dylan doesn't know how much more yet.

Still, he's going to take what he can get, and right now that's Brendan pressed close to his side, his arm around his waist, and his fingers tucked under his belt. It's not a bad arrangement, even if nothing else happens, and Dylan is going to be happy with that.

"This is Brendan," he says, nodding at the man next to him. "My roommate. Brendan, this is Jon Hutchins, my mentor."

"Mentor?" Brendan gives Dylan a pointed look. "In what?"

"What do you think? Leatherwork!"

It doesn't take long for Brendan to pull back from Dylan just enough to shoot him an incredulous look. "You're giving *me* a hard time because I didn't tell you about or show you my metalwork, and you're a leatherworker? You do this kind of thing?" He waves his hand over Jon's table.

"Well, not quite this good, but yeah, basically."

"What do you mean, *not quite this good*?" Jon shakes his head and looks straight at Brendan. "His stuff is great; he just doesn't want to admit it."

"I'll have to take your word for it. He hasn't shown me any of it."

"You haven't shown me any of your stuff either!"

"We'll have show and tell when we get back to the room," Brendan says dryly, rolling his eyes before returning his attention to Jon. "So you taught him everything he knows?"

"Well, everything he knows about leatherwork. I refuse to take responsibility for his knowledge—or lack thereof—in other areas." Jon leans in close and winks at Brendan. "Getting him to grasp the leatherworking bits was hard enough. I despair for his poor parents and teachers."

"I'm standing right here, you know."

"Of course." Jon grins widely. "It's more fun that way. Wouldn't be sporting if you weren't here."

"Great." Dylan rolls his eyes. "Nice to know you care."

"Of course I do." He comes around the table and slides his arm over Dylan's shoulder. "You are my favorite student. Even if you are hopeless."

Dylan tries to twist away, but Brendan holds him tight—something he wouldn't object to any other time—and he's stuck, sandwiched between them as they banter back and forth like old friends, ragging on Dylan. Whatever Brendan might have been like when he'd first met Tara, he's not shy now, at least not when he's around Dylan. It's somewhat worrisome, actually. Dylan is sure that Jon knows things he would rather Brendan didn't find out just yet, and he *knows* that Brendan is aware of things that Jon does *not* need to know. Their activities this morning, for example.

"So," Jon says when he finally pulls away and walks back around his table. His eyes dart between the two of them and his lips curve up into a smile that makes Dylan just a little nervous. "Did you two coordinate today?"

"What? No! Brendan isn't even a pirate! He's a character from *Stardust*!"

"The one who was given that outfit by a pirate? What's his name, Tristan?"

"Trist*ran*," Dylan corrects, immediately flushing. He should not be worried about Jon getting the character name for Brendan's costume correct. "He told me a lot on Friday, all right? This is the second day he's worn that costume, and it's sunk into my head!"

"Uh-huh." Jon looks dubious. "If you say so."

"I do!" Dylan risks a glance at Brendan. "It's not my fault he has to reuse costumes."

"And you won't?" Jon gives Dylan a stern look. "What are you wearing tomorrow?"

"This, probably, but—"

"And you *drove*," Brendan flashes an all-too-innocent grin. "I happen to like this costume, and most of it is my pirate outfit, anyway. The coat and vest are more fun than the hat and scarves, though, so I'm wearing it until the party tonight."

Dylan mentally changes Brendan's coat for the pirate hat sitting on top of the television in their room and several bright scarves. The coat *is* nicer, he has to admit, and the whole idea works well with the limited packing space Brendan had since he was flying. Dylan isn't just going to admit that, though. "And tomorrow?" he asks instead, his eyebrow raised.

"Maybe this." Brendan shrugs. "Maybe Crowley. We'll see."

Either costume is perfectly okay with Dylan, though at this point Brendan could probably wear rags and Dylan would find it attractive.

He's got it bad, and his face flushes just thinking about Brendan in that nicely tailored suit again. "Oh." It's hardly an adequate response, but it's all he can manage at the moment.

"Yeah. *Oh*." Brendan's tone is light and teasing, and he grins as he starts to tug Dylan away. "It was nice to meet you, Jon. I'm sure we'll be back around later."

Jon clasps them both on the shoulder. "You two have fun."

"Will do," Dylan manages as they walk away. He's a little distracted at the moment, and he's definitely going to have to head back to the Art Show again later, without Brendan, if he wants to seriously look at anything that's left. They walk past it all, stopping a few times, but Dylan doesn't see anything but the images Jon and Brendan managed to put into his mind.

They're probably a lot nicer, anyway. The art is amazing, but nothing can beat what he's imagining.

TIM sidles up to Brendan, slinging an arm over his shoulders and grinning maniacally. "So. You and Dylan, huh?"

"Me and Dylan what?" Brendan asks after a minute, raising his eyebrows as he looks at his friend. He has a pretty good idea what Tim is talking about, but Matt isn't here to rein in Tim's enthusiasm yet, so Brendan is going to make him work for every bit of information. Besides, he remembers what Tim and Matt were like when they first got together, and how glad everyone was when it happened, and how they tried so hard to keep their little secret for as long as possible. Brendan isn't above getting payback, even four years later.

"You know." Tim waves his free hand in front of them. "You and Dylan."

"Right." Brendan draws out the word. "What about us?"

"Is there an us? Er, a you? Never mind." Tim shakes his head and swings around so he's facing Brendan, both his hands on Brendan's shoulders. "Are you and Dylan? You know."

"Uh, no. I don't."

"Come on man!" Tim looks around, his eyes comically wide, and leans in close to Brendan's ear. "I'd let you wait until after dinner, but I'm going to have to cut out early. I'm doing the Thriller Dance. You gotta tell me now."

"Tell you what?" Brendan carefully assumes his most innocent expression. He won't be able to hold out much longer or Tim will lose the small bit of decorum he possesses and blurt out something vaguely obscene—and very private—loud enough for everyone in the restaurant to hear, but he's going to get every bit of enjoyment out of this that he possibly can.

"About you and Dylan!"

"What about Brendan and Dylan?" Kevin clasps Tim on the shoulder and turns an expectant look at Brendan. "Did the two of you finally *do* something?" he asks in lieu of a greeting.

"We've *done* lots of things," Brendan replies, shooting a glare at both Tim and Kevin before turning to Laura, who's holding Kevin's hand and watching them all with an amused expression. "Hey, Laura."

"Hey," she responds, grinning as she leans in to kiss Brendan on the cheek. "Just ignore my husband here, yeah?"

"I always do."

"Hey!" Kevin hits Brendan on the shoulder with a loose fist, knocking him free of Tim's grasp.

Brendan takes the opportunity to move behind Laura, using her as a shield against both Tim and Kevin. It's something more in character for someone half his age, but he has no qualms about it if it keeps him safe from his so-called friends. "I'll tell you whatever you want to know if you stay in front of me," he whispers in Laura's ear as he takes her shoulders and moves her so she's in the best position to keep him somewhat safe.

Her eyes sparkle as she looks over her shoulder at him. "*Everything* I want to know?"

"Yeah! Just—" Brendan maneuvers her around as Kevin moves, keeping her between them.

"Deal." Laura flashes a grin at Brendan before directing her attention to Tim and Kevin. "Now, boys," she says in a deceitfully pleasant tone, "I know you want to have a nice dinner, so let's behave, okay?" The last word is emphasized with a raised eyebrow that gets both Tim and Kevin to nod furiously.

They're still nodding when Matt comes up, wraps his arms around Tim's waist, and rests his chin on his shoulder. "Laura whipping everyone into shape?"

"Of course. That *is* my job," she replies, slipping her arm around Kevin's waist and leaning her head on his shoulder.

It's a casual move, one that Brendan has seen her make hundreds of times, but this time it leaves him feeling like the odd man out. Usually Nate is at their Sunday night dinners, too, and since they've both been single for years they act as each other's date for the night. It leads to lots of inappropriate jokes and the night usually ends with both of them remembering why they would never actually date the other, but this year it's just Brendan, and it stings a little more than he expected.

He pushes the feeling aside, determined to have a good time anyway, and shakes his head at Matt. "I'm not sure even *she* can keep these two in line."

"He only says that because we were giving him a hard time about *Dylan*," Tim grouses, leaning back against Matt.

"What about Dylan?"

"That's what we want to know." Kevin narrows his eyes and mock glares at Brendan. "Apparently, Brendan doesn't kiss and tell, though."

"Who says I've kissed him?" It comes out in a squeaky voice, completely blowing any chance he had of deflecting their interest, and it's only the host calling his name to let him know that their table is ready that saves him from further interrogation.

The reprieve only lasts as long as it takes to get to their table. As soon as they're seated, four sets of eyes home in on him. Laura puts her hand on his arm, all the charm that kept Kevin and Tim at bay earlier now directed at him. "So, Brendan," she asks in a scarily sweet tone. "What *have* you and Dylan been up to?"

Brendan gulps. It's going to be a very *long* dinner.

DYLAN bounces his leg up and down until Sabrina puts a stop to it by pressing her palm to his knee and looking at him coyly. "He's not going to vanish over dinner, Dylan."

"Oh, I know." Dylan blinks, shakes his head, and blinks again, this time going for a more innocent look. "I mean, what? Who?"

"Funny." Kelly shakes her head from across the table. She looks a little demented with her fork poised over her plate, but her smile is affectionate, and Dylan is almost positive that she won't stab anything but her food. "It's obvious you can't stand to be parted from the guy. You could at least do him the favor of admitting it."

Dylan thinks about denying it, asking whom they're talking about, or telling them that there's no one he can't stand to be apart from, but the looks on their faces stop him. They both know, somehow, even though this is the first time he's seen them since things with Brendan progressed past blow jobs, and Dylan started thinking that he might want to see more of Brendan than just being here at Dragon*Con allows. He's not sure *how* they know, but they both clearly do, so there's no point in even trying to lie.

"Shut up," he mumbles, stabbing hard at his chicken and glaring at Kelly from beneath lowered eyelids. He can feel his cheeks flushing, growing redder the more he thinks about Brendan, but it's not as though he can just stop thinking about him. He's pretty sure he's not capable at this point, and positive that he doesn't want to even if he could.

"Awww," Sabrina croons, her fingers brushing against Dylan's arm as she pulls back, "Dylan's in *love*."

"I said *shut up!*"

The girls freeze, staring at him with wide eyes and open mouths. "Oh. My. God!" Kelly finally exclaims, her hand flying up to cover her mouth. "You *are* in love with him!"

"I am not!" The protest sounds weak even to Dylan, and he knows he's not in love with Brendan, but he pushes on anyway. There's no way to make it sound better. "I've only known him for three days! I can't be!"

"Okay, so you're in lust or like or *something* with him, then." Kelly's grin widens, making her look positively evil. "I mean, come on, Dylan, you don't blush like that just because you think a guy is cute. I *know* that."

She has a point, but that doesn't mean Dylan is going to concede easily. "So?"

"*So,*" Sabrina mimics, "it's sweet."

"And cute."

"*Adorable.*"

"What are you going to do about it, Dylan?"

He feels like he's at a tennis match watching the two of them banter back and forth. When they turn to look at him, both directing wide eyes and bright smiles his way, he freezes. "Nothing?"

"Dylan!" they exclaim in unison, both leaning in and widening their eyes as they stare at him.

"What?" He looks between them with a defiant expression on his face. It's moderately better than his terrified one. "What am I supposed to do? I hardly know him—"

"Which is the whole point of dating him."

Dylan glares at Sabrina and raises his voice. "He lives over four hours away—"

"Which is closer than your last boyfriend and half of your friends."

He switches his glare to Kelly and raises his voice once more. "And I don't know if he's even remotely interested," he finishes, practically yelling so they can't talk over him.

"Ask!"

"It's really, *really* creepy when you two do that, you know," Dylan tells them, looking first at Kelly and then at Sabrina. "It's kind of frightening, really."

They look at each other, sharing identical grins, and turn back to Dylan with mischievous expressions on their faces. "We know."

Dylan shudders and cowers dramatically, hiding behind his hands. "Stop it!"

"Make us!"

He pushes his chair back, but Sabrina grabs his arm and tugs him back down. "Sit down, Dylan."

"But—"

"Oh come on, do you really think we can keep that up for very long?" She shakes her head and giggles. "I mean, really, Dylan. Kelly and I may share a brain sometimes, but we don't talk together all that often."

"Often enough," he murmurs as he sits back down, shooting a glare at both of them for good measure before picking up his fork again and stabbing at his plate.

"Seriously, Dylan," Kelly says after a few minutes. "You should talk to him about it. Maybe he's thinking the same thing and is worried about what you'll say?"

It's a good point, but that doesn't mean that Dylan is going to act on it. "I'm not even sure I want to do anything once Dragon*Con is over." He shrugs and puts a piece of chicken in his mouth, chewing it completely before he continues. "Maybe it's better to not say anything."

Sabrina looks at him sadly. "Is that what you really think?"

"I don't know." Dylan shrugs. "There are plenty of reasons not to say anything."

"And the reason to say something trumps them all."

"I'm not in love with him, Kelly."

"That's not what I meant."

"Then what?" Dylan tilts his head to the side, resting his chin on his hands as he awaits her answer. "What else could possibly be the reason?"

"Because you *could* fall in love with him. He makes you happy, Dylan. I haven't seen you moon over someone like this since you and Justin broke up! It's nice to see you like this. Really."

"Yeah, well." Dylan shrugs again. "I don't know. Maybe I just need a fling."

"Fling?"

"Yes! Is there something wrong with that?"

Sabrina frowns. "Well, no, not if you're both consenting adults, but that just doesn't seem like you, Dylan."

"Maybe it is."

"Dylan…."

"Look, can we just not talk about it? I'm not going to do anything today, anyway, no matter what, so it's a moot point, all right?"

"Just promise you'll think about it, okay, Dylan?" Sabrina lays a hand on his forearm and squeezes gently. "I'd hate for you to pass this opportunity up because you don't have the balls to act on it."

He can't keep the serious attitude any longer, so he pulls back his arm and grins wickedly. "Oh, I have the balls, sweetheart. Wanna see?"

"Like you'd actually show me."

"Care to place a wager on that?" He stands and starts to unbuckle his belt, wiggling his hips and winking ludicrously the whole time. People at nearby tables are watching with wide eyes, but Dylan doesn't care. He's not planning to get far.

"Stop!" Sabrina grabs his hands and tugs them away before he manages to get the belt unbuckled. "I don't want to go blind!"

Dylan drops back into his chair, presses his hand to his heart, and lets his head flop back as he sags. "Oh, the pain! I'm heartbroken!"

"Shut up." Kelly kicks at him, her tiny feet hitting rather ineffectively against his knee-high boots. She's too far away to do any real damage. "You are not, and you know it."

"Am too!"

"No, you're not." Sabrina grabs his shirt and pulls him back upright. "Now stop acting like a baby and finish your dinner."

"Yes, *Mom*." He dodges Sabrina's swinging arm, grins, and asks about her day. He'll tell them about Tara and about what Jon said later. Much later.

BRENDAN is running late. He stayed longer at dinner than he'd originally planned, and now he has to hurry back to the room and change before heading to the Pirate Party. He *could* go dressed in his Tristran costume—it is a pirate costume of sorts, after all—but it seems a waste to do so when all he has to do is ditch the coat and vest and add on a hat and a few scarves to look more like a *real* pirate. Or Hollywood's version of a real pirate, anyway. Actual real pirates probably didn't wear anything nearly as nice as what Brendan is planning to wear back in the time period he's supposed to be representing, and he's almost certain that modern pirates dress like every other modern seafarer.

He gets to the Marriott elevator bays just in time to see Dylan step inside the one that goes to their floor, but before he can get there, the doors close, and Dylan either doesn't see or hear him, or the elevator is too full to hold, because he doesn't stop them. Brendan makes a lunge for the button, but before he can get to it, the elevator going up to the set of floors above theirs opens, and he jumps in, jabbing the button for the tenth floor and sighing gratefully when it closes after only one other person gets on.

The ride to the tenth floor is fast, as the elevator can't stop along the way. After it leaves the Atrium, Lobby, and Lounge levels, it can stop at the tenth floor because of the lounge there, but then it can't stop at any other floor before it gets to its set. It's a complicated system, though it does keep people on the highest floors from having to stop at every floor beneath theirs, but Brendan's room leaves him uniquely positioned to use the tenth-floor trick

When the doors open, Brendan dashes out and heads straight for the spiral stairs heading up to eleven. If he's timed it right, he should be able to catch Dylan just as he's getting off the elevator, and they can head down to the Pirate Party together after he changes.

It doesn't quite work out that way, though.

Apparently, Dylan's elevator didn't make many stops below eleven, because he's already halfway down the hall when Brendan gets to the top of the steps. Brendan doesn't even think. He just shouts Dylan's name and runs, his long coat flying out behind him as he tears down the hallway, his boots thudding hard against the carpeted floor, and his sword swinging wildly in its sheath.

He's sure he looks ridiculous, and he can't even explain why it's so important that he gets to Dylan before Dylan gets to their room, but he doesn't stop to think about it, he just runs, his legs pumping and his chest heaving as he dashes down the hallway.

Dylan is waiting, watching with wide eyes when Brendan reaches him and stops, leaning over and resting his hands on his knees as he gasps for breath. He's not in as good a shape as he thought he was, because that short dash has left him feeling horribly winded, but he reached Dylan before Dylan got inside, so he's counting it as a victory, even if his lungs and leg muscles are not. Their votes don't really count anyway.

Not when his heart is involved.

Dylan raises an eyebrow as Brendan skids to a stop and leans back against the railing that circles the open area in the middle of the hotel. It's designed so it would take a significant amount of effort to get over it and fall to the Atrium Level below, but it still makes Brendan's heart skip a beat when he sees Dylan leaning back, his arms spread wide and braced against the top of the half-wall that surrounds the hallway on the open side.

It's ridiculous, really. Brendan *knows* Dylan won't fall, but he can't stop himself from grabbing Dylan's shirt and tugging him forward, catching his lips in a bruising kiss that leaves him feeling even more breathless before pulling back and grinning widely, his fingers still fisted in Dylan's shirt. "Hi."

"Hey." Dylan's grin matches Brendan's, and though confusion is evident in his eyes, he doesn't object when Brendan threads their fingers together and tugs Dylan down the rest of the hallway to their room.

They're inside, and Brendan is standing in front of the closet, hanging up his jacket and vest as he tries to decide if he needs to send his suit out for dry cleaning so he can wear it tomorrow or if it will be okay as-is, when Dylan wraps his arms around his waist and leans his chin on his shoulder. "You want to tell me what that was about?"

Brendan shrugs as he turns in Dylan's arms. "Don't know, really. I just really wanted to get to you before you got to the room."

"Why?"

"So we can go to the Pirate Party together?"

"And that's it?"

"Yeah?" He shrugs again. "I didn't think, you know? I saw you get on that elevator and just really wanted to catch up with you."

"So, what, you took another elevator up to ten and then ran the rest of the way?"

"Pretty much."

Brendan isn't sure what he expected Dylan's response to be, but it wasn't leaning in and kissing him soundly before pulling back and bopping his nose with his index finger. "That's adorable."

"It's not creepy or weird?"

Dylan takes a step back, puts his hands on Brendan's shoulders, and eyes him for a minute. "Well, maybe a little. But it's mostly adorable."

Brendan wrinkles his nose. That wasn't what he was going for, though it definitely beats creepy, or desperate, or weird, so he supposes that he shouldn't argue with it too much. He can't just let it slide, though. His pride is at stake. "Really? *Adorable*?"

"Yep. Adorable. It's okay, though," Dylan adds as he leans in, grinning. "I like adorable."

As he presses his lips to Brendan's, kissing him soundly, Brendan decides that if this is the kind of response it gets, he likes adorable too, pride be dammed.

DYLAN wraps his arm around Brendan as they stagger out of the Pirate Party. They're tipsy, though not drunk like last night—and wow is Dylan glad *that* turned out the way it did, because *boy* could that have been awkward—but there's enough alcohol in Dylan's system that he doesn't hesitate to sling his arm over Brendan's shoulders and hold him close the entire way back to their room.

Brendan doesn't seem to mind. He's not leaning heavily the way he was after the Party of Loathing, but there's a small smile on his face as he slips his arm around Dylan's waist, pressing himself close as he matches his steps to Dylan's.

It's nice, more than nice, actually, and as they're walking, Dylan considers ignoring all the reasons talking to Brendan about what he thinks he might want is a bad idea and just blurting out the question. Then he starts to imagine all the ways it could go wrong, and how awkward the rest of the convention could be, and he clamps his mouth shut so tightly that his teeth start to hurt.

By the time they get to the room, Dylan's jaw is twitching with the effort of not saying anything, and Brendan looks at him oddly as he slides the keycard into the door. "You okay?"

"Fine," Dylan says, pulling his arm from around Brendan's shoulder as they step into the room. Walking back to the room like that is one thing—Dylan is an overly affectionate guy, and he has friends here who will attest to that if asked—but staying like that once they're in the privacy of their hotel room would be awkward. They're just two guys who have had sex a couple of times, not soul mates or anything crazy like that.

Brendan's eyes widen and his jaw drops open slightly. "Are you sure?" He tilts his head to the side, looking at Dylan critically, and shakes it. "You don't look fine. You look constipated. You're not constipated, are you? I don't think I have anything for that."

"Um. No?" Dylan isn't sure where that came from, but a small part of him is relieved to know that his brain isn't the only one that gets off track sometimes.

"Oh. Good." Brendan tosses his hat on the bed and begins taking off his accessories. "So then what's wrong?" He asks, turning with his belt half undone, his hands frozen at his waist holding it up. "Your jaw has been twitching since we got on the elevator, and I'm almost positive that's not normal."

Dylan freezes. Fuck. He didn't realize Brendan had noticed, not that he could have done anything about it even if he had. The only other option is to blurt everything out, and that's not an option, no matter what his friends say. "It has?" he asks in a strained voice. He was going for nonchalant, but he's too tense to pull it off and the attempt just makes him sound even more uptight than he actually is.

"Yeah." Brendan finishes taking off his belt and sets it on the bed carefully before crossing the room to stand in front of Dylan. He gently pulls Dylan's hands down, holding them in his, and looks him straight in the eyes. His expression is so tender and concerned that it makes Dylan's heart skip a beat as he wonders what Brendan could possibly be imagining is wrong. "So what's the issue?"

"There isn't one!" Dylan tries to tug his hands free so he can wave them around, but Brendan holds them firm. The inability to move them just makes Dylan more nervous, and he starts babbling. "I swear, Brendan, there's nothing wrong. I'm fine. You're fine. We're fine."

"*We're* fine?" Brendan's eyes twinkle and his lips curve into an amused smile. "Is that so?"

"I... hope so?"

"You do?"

"Y-yes?" Dylan keeps expecting Brendan to run screaming, but instead he just grins wider, which leaves Dylan feeling extremely nervous. "Is that okay?"

"More than," Brendan whispers as he slides his hands up Dylan's arms and pulls him down for a kiss.

His lips are soft against Dylan's, parted just enough for Dylan to slip his tongue inside, and soon they're kissing passionately, their tongues dancing as their fingers clench in each other's hair, and their bodies plaster together. Brendan pushes Dylan down onto the bed and climbs on his lap, straddling his hips as he leans in, deepening the kiss and rubbing his groin against Dylan's in a way that leaves no doubt as to his intentions.

Dylan moans, his hips moving up reflexively, but his brain finishes processing their earlier words, catches up to what's going on, and calls an immediate halt to all activities. Dylan needs to know what they're doing before he can do this again. "What are we doing?" he asks, pulling back just enough that he can look Brendan in the eyes.

"Making out?" Brendan's eyes grow wide. "You're not *that* drunk, are you? I didn't think you had that many tonight!" He pushes back and starts to climb off Dylan.

"Not drunk," Dylan tells him, grabbing his arms and pulling him back down. "Just tipsy."

Brendan warily lowers himself back onto Dylan's lap. "Okay," he draws out the word, making it clear that he doesn't quite believe what he's hearing, but that he's willing to go along with it for the moment.

"I didn't mean what are we doing *right now*," Dylan clarifies, his hands still around Brendan's upper arms. He's not letting go until they've worked this out. "I meant in general. I mean, we hardly know each other, and I don't know if we'll see each other after the convention is over and—"

Brendan cuts him off with a finger over his lips. "Do you want to?"

"I think, but—"

"Then we will." He shrugs and leans in, putting his lips right against Dylan's ear. "We don't have to make any promises to see each other again when this is over."

"I know."

"So what's the problem?" Brendan pulls back and frowns at Dylan with a puzzled expression on his face. "You like what we're doing, right? You like me?"

"Yes...." Dylan isn't sure where Brendan is going with this, and he's afraid he's not going to like it.

"Good. I like what we're doing, and I like you. So as long as that doesn't change, we can figure things out as we go along."

"But you live in Buffalo!"

"West Seneca, actually, but so? Why does that matter?"

"I live in Albany!"

"Dylan." Brendan cups Dylan's chin with one hand and looks him straight in the eyes. "We're not anywhere close to the cohabitation stage of a relationship yet. We can keep in touch other ways, like this new-fangled internet thing. I think you've heard of it?"

"Shut up." Dylan relaxes his grip on Brendan's arms, and relief floods his body. It's not the answer he was looking for, not really, but it *is* a better answer than the one he was expecting, and he's not going to argue with that. At least not yet. He'll work on getting a better answer from Brendan later.

Maybe.

For now, he's going to go with this and enjoy it.

"Why don't you make me?" Brendan asks, wriggling his hips and rubbing his groin against Dylan's.

It's an excellent idea, and Dylan grins as he pulls Brendan in for another kiss.

MONDAY

WHEN Brendan wakes up, he's wrapped around Dylan, his head pillowed on Dylan's chest and his leg slung over Dylan's hip. It's the most comfortable he's been upon awakening in longer than he can remember, and he sighs contentedly as he nuzzles closer, a happy smile on his face. He absently presses a kiss to Dylan's shoulder as he moves, and Dylan responds by making a pleased noise and briefly squeezing Brendan. He doesn't open his eyes, though, and his muscles relax completely as the squeeze ends, leaving no sign he stirred at all. It's endearing, and Brendan smiles as he lets his eyes drift closed.

It's the perfect morning, lying here dozing lazily in their bed, all warm and happy and tangled together. Brendan doesn't want it to end, which means that the thought is tainted as soon as he thinks it. He only has one more morning to wake up like this in *their* bed, and despite what he told Dylan last night, Brendan isn't sure he's okay with that.

It seems ridiculous, because they barely know each other at all, but Brendan is going to miss Dylan a lot when they leave tomorrow, and he really, *really* hopes that they're able to make this work once they're over four hours apart and outside the protective bubble of Dragon*Con. Things have been practically perfect while they've been here, and Brendan hates to think that the real world will ruin that.

He can't let it.

Nor can he actually admit that he's feeling that way to anyone except *maybe* Dylan, and he's not completely certain about that. He should, and he knows it, but despite Dylan's confession last night, he's not ready to admit his own worries. They reached a conclusion that left them both almost satisfied, and if Brendan is going to work much harder than he implied to make sure that this works, well, no one really needs to know that.

Right?

It's not something he wants to ponder right now, anyway. There are only a few more minutes before his phone will start beeping at him, telling him he needs to get up and face the day, and there's so much that he needs and wants to do that he's not even sure he's looking forward to it. He wants to spend time lounging in the room with Dylan, but he needs to swing through the Dealers Room, Exhibit Hall, and Art Show this morning to pick up a few things he didn't buy on his previous visits, assuming they're still available. He wants to meet up with Kevin, Tim, and Matt, together or separately, and spend a little time with them before they part ways for at least several more months. And, most importantly, he needs to get a few hours alone someplace private for his own special little project.

That is going to be the challenge. He doesn't want to tell any of his friends what he's doing, and he can't risk doing it in the room or Dylan might walk in and see, and that would be disastrous. It's most important that Dylan have no idea what Brendan is up to until it's completely done.

Arranging his day is going to be a challenge.

He's drifting off to sleep again, planning to milk those last few wonderful minutes for all they're worth, when Dylan stirs beneath him, blinking his eyes open and grinning sleepily. "Morning."

"Morning," Brendan replies, tilting his head up to meet Dylan's lips in a gentle kiss. "Sleep well?"

"Amazingly." Dylan extends his arms up in the air, groaning and arching his back a little as he stretches. "I need to sleep with you wrapped around me more often."

Brendan makes an absentminded sound of agreement. "We'll have to see what we can do about that," he murmurs, not thinking about what he's saying or how Dylan will take it. He means it, though, with every fiber of his being.

Dylan slowly stills beneath him, his muscles gradually growing tense under Brendan's touch as his hand stops making circles on Brendan's back. "You mean that?" It's barely a whisper, so quiet that it's mostly just noise and not words, and Brendan has to concentrate hard to pick out what Dylan said.

"Of course." He lifts his head and gazes down at Dylan. "Look, man, I meant what I said last night. We're both happy with this, right?" He pauses and waits for Dylan to nod before continuing. "Then let's not question it, okay?"

"Yeah, but—"

Brendan cuts Dylan off with a finger on his lips. "Stop worrying so much. I like waking up wrapped around you. You like waking up with me wrapped around you. So we'll both do what we can to make sure that it happens again after tomorrow. Okay?"

"Yeah." Dylan slides his hand up Brendan's back and over his neck to cup his head and pull him down for a kiss. This one is neither gentle nor swift, and Brendan sinks himself into it, slipping his tongue into Dylan's mouth and curling it, sliding it along Dylan's as they lose themselves in the kiss.

It takes several blissful minutes for them to pull apart, and when they do, Brendan rests his forehead against Dylan's and grins as he pants and looks straight into Dylan's eyes. "Hi."

"Hey."

That's all it takes. Brendan lowers his lips, Dylan shifts his leg, and then they're rubbing their groins together as they kiss, their bodies moving as one, and if Brendan were even remotely capable of thinking rationally, he'd be worried about what was going to happen to the sheets. Again.

He isn't, however, so he doesn't care at all.

He doesn't care about anything except the way Dylan is moving under him and around him, touching him everywhere he can reach as he twists his tongue in a way that leaves Brendan reeling for more. "God, Dylan," he gasps as he pulls back for air. "Need…."

"Yeah." Dylan rolls them over, pinning Brendan to the bed and grinning down at him. "Can I…?" He trails off without finishing the question, but Brendan can see it in his eyes, can feel it in the way his hips are pressing against Brendan's, and can hear it in the soft want in his voice.

"Yeah." It's not something Brendan does very often—he's usually the one in control in the few relationships he's had—but he wants this, wants to give in to Dylan and let him be in control, even if it's just this once. He doesn't like thinking it, but he might never have another chance to let Dylan do this, and he can't stand the thought of leaving Atlanta without giving this to Dylan, without *getting* this from Dylan. It's suddenly as important as doing everything he can to make sure that they do see each other again after they go their separate ways tomorrow morning. "*Please*," he adds, looking straight into Dylan's eyes and putting everything he feels into his gaze.

Dylan's gaze darkens as he stares down at Brendan. "Really?" It's more of an awed exclamation than a question, and Brendan can't help but grin as he watches Dylan's face light up when he realizes that Brendan is serious.

"Yes, really," he says, a teasing lilt to his voice that's belied by the desire in his gaze and the intensity with which he pulls Dylan down for another kiss. He loses himself in it, sliding his tongue deeply into Dylan's mouth and scratching his fingers down his back. It's crazy, and passionate, and everything that Brendan wants to have forever and always. It's perfect, which is even crazier, because perfect doesn't exist, and he's only known Dylan for three days.

When he finally pulls back, Dylan stretches over Brendan and grabs the supplies from the bedside table. He's positioned between

Brendan's knees, resting back on his heels, before Brendan even processes that he has moved, but when he slides a slicked finger into Brendan's ass, Brendan stops worrying about how it happened and starts concentrating on what Dylan is doing to him, and how it's making him feel.

It's fantastic, marvelous, wonderful, every good word Brendan can possibly think of. Dylan's finger is long and thick, and Brendan is grateful, because he's seen the size of Dylan's cock. Dylan twists it around, hitting Brendan in that spot that leaves him reeling and gasping as he struggles not to buck his hips. Another finger joins the first, and then a third, and soon Brendan is so lost in the sensation that he can hardly do anything other than lie on his back, moaning and writhing as Dylan stretches him open.

When Dylan pulls out, Brendan is left blinking, gasping for breath and too close to the edge to do anything other than watch through hooded eyes as Dylan slides the condom over his cock, stretching it out almost as far as it will go and slicking himself with the lube. It's the hottest thing Brendan has ever seen, and though he would like to be the one preparing Dylan, he's not going to object to the show, either. If he has to watch and not participate, at least he has something good to focus on.

Brendan can't decide if Dylan finishes too soon or not soon enough, but then Dylan is moving again, lifting Brendan's legs and positioning himself at Brendan's entrance. He leans forward before he pushes, holding himself up over Brendan's body with his hands, and makes sure he catches Brendan's eye before he thrusts.

It's incredible. Dylan is bigger than anyone Brendan has ever been with before, but it feels so right. Brendan's whole body feels full to the brim, and though it's not without pain—Dylan is a giant, after all, and he pushed himself all the way in with one thrust—it's the good kind that Brendan knows is leading to something fabulous. "Oh God," he manages, staring up at Dylan with wide eyes as he clenches his fists in the sheets and waits for his body to adjust.

"Is it too much?" Dylan moves as though he's going to pull back. "I can—"

"No!" Brendan would grab Dylan, but he can't make himself let go of the sheets just yet, so he tries to put everything he's feeling into his tone. "Just... just give me a minute." He smiles up at Dylan. "You're kinda bigger than I'm used to. And it's been a while."

"For me too," Dylan admits. "Well, until Friday night, anyway," he adds with a small, fond smile. He looks about ready to babble, and it's sweet, but Brendan has other plans for the next several minutes.

"Okay," he whispers, letting his fingers relax around the sheets and deliberately clenching his buttocks. "Move."

Dylan cuts off mid-thought, his eyes widening and his grin growing. "You sure?"

"Yes!" Brendan grabs Dylan's arms and pulls him down until their noses are practically touching. It changes the angle of his cock slightly, eliciting a hiss of both pleasure and pain from Brendan, but he ignores it and focuses on getting through to Dylan. "*Move.*"

Dylan blinks, grins, and pulls back slightly. This time when he thrusts forward, it's faster, harder, and with just the right angle to leave Brendan seeing stars. "God, Brendan," he pants as he moves, pulling back and thrusting in repeatedly, sending jolts of pleasure through Brendan's body with each push. Brendan moves his hand between them, grabbing his own cock and stroking it in time with Dylan's thrusts. He wishes it could be Dylan's hand stroking him, enveloping him fully with its width, and then it is, as Dylan gently pushes Brendan's hand away and takes over, balancing himself up on one arm.

Brendan pulls him down further, capturing his lips in a searing kiss, and it's while their tongues are entwined that he comes, gasping Dylan's name into his mouth and clenching around Dylan's cock. Dylan follows suit, spilling his seed into the condom as Brendan shakes around him, calling out Brendan's name as he throws back his head and collapsing in a boneless heap on top of him when he's done.

It is several minutes before Brendan has the strength to think about moving, and even then, he's too comfortable to really want to do so. It's not until Dylan yawns and snuffles closer that Brendan moves at all, pushing lightly against Dylan's shoulders and coaxing him to roll off and pull out so that Brendan can get something to clean them both up.

He hurries into the bathroom, moving slower than he hoped but faster than he honestly expected, and wets one of the washcloths before returning to the bed, and to Dylan. Dylan is almost asleep when Brendan climbs back on, and he barely stirs as Brendan wipes him down, making sure he's clean and that the condom is disposed of before carefully wiping the sticky white fluid from his own cock and lower stomach. He really should take a shower, but it's early still, and Dylan looks so comfortable and inviting that Brendan just climbs back into bed after dropping the washcloth in the sink, wrapping himself back around Dylan and letting himself enjoy a few more minutes of this wonderful morning.

He's going to have to face the day soon enough, and though he's looking forward to the things he has planned, it's also a bittersweet thought. The last day of Dragon*Con always is.

Brendan will happily take the distraction of curling up with Dylan for as long as he's able.

DYLAN doesn't want to get out of bed. He's got Brendan wrapped around him, he's comfortable and content, and if he moves, he's going to have to acknowledge that today is the last day of Dragon*Con, his last chance to spend any real time with Brendan. Sure, they'll have tomorrow morning, but they won't be able to be lazy. Brendan will have to leave early to catch his flight, and Dylan will have to make sure he gets everything packed up in time to take MARTA to the garage, retrieve his car, and still make it back before check-out time.

It's not going to be a fun morning, and he'll spend most of it away from Brendan, an idea he already doesn't like, though he's going to have to get used to it.

Not quite yet, though. They still have this morning, and this afternoon, and they definitely have tonight.

Dylan fully intends to make the most of tonight, in every way possible.

First, however, he has to get through the day, and he plans to spend as much of that with Brendan as he can. He just isn't sure how well that's going to work. He needs to do a few things without Brendan—work on the project he started the other day after the parade, and swing by Tara's table in the Dealers Room to pick up a few things—and then there are a few panels he'd like to attend if he can manage to motivate himself, and he really does need to spend a little time with Kelly, Sabrina, and his other friends. It's going to be complicated trying to get everything to work out, but Dylan is determined to try.

It will be worth it if he can succeed.

As he's pondering the best way to work out his schedule, Brendan stirs, snuffling into Dylan's shoulder for a minute before slowly opening his eyes and blinking at him. He's definitely not fully awake yet, and, as he looks at Dylan, trying to figure out where he is and why, Dylan can't resist kissing his forehead.

"Good morning," he says, grinning as Brendan's brow furrows with further confusion. "Sleep well?"

Brendan scrunches up his nose, looking for all the world like that's the most unreasonable question he's ever been asked, and buries his face in Dylan's shoulder again. "Can I get back to you on that?"

It's somewhat ridiculous, as this is the second time they've woken up, and Brendan really has no excuses for still being so tired, but it's also charming, so Dylan just runs his fingers through

Brendan's hair and shakes his head. "We need to get up soon," he says quietly, kissing Brendan's forehead again.

Brendan's eyes open again and he squints up at Dylan. "Why?"

"Places to go, people to see, things to do?"

"Can't one of those things be sleep in?

"Well, it could," Dylan agrees amiably, "but I think we've already done that. It's after ten."

Brendan wrinkles his nose again, but he grudgingly rubs at his eyes and pushes back the covers. Dylan knows from their mornings together that he's going to take a while to get out of bed, so he slips out from under him, starts the complimentary coffee in the coffeemaker, and heads in to the shower.

Part of him is hoping that Brendan will join him, simply because he knows where it will lead, and he leaves the door open in invitation, but there's another part of his brain that doesn't want Brendan to accept it, simply because he knows where it will lead. Shower sex would be awesome, and Dylan makes a mental note to try to squeeze it in today if he can, but if he wants to make any of the panels he was thinking about attending, he can't afford to get caught up in Brendan again. They'll never get out of the room.

He's not sure that's a bad thing, and that thought scares him more than a little.

Dylan hasn't been in a relationship for years, hasn't wanted one, thanks to the way the last one ended, and now he's feeling all these things and thinking all these crazy thoughts about not wanting to spend time away from Brendan, and it's scary. More than scary. He's never fallen this quickly before, and a big part of him is afraid that he's going to get his heart broken when Dragon*Con is over, despite what Brendan said last night and this morning.

They were just words, after all, and Dylan is afraid that Brendan will change his mind once he's back in the real world, away from the magic and lure of Dragon*Con. Things are different here, marvelous and wonderful, and Dylan is afraid that whatever happens with the two of them after they leave Atlanta, it won't compare to here. He's afraid it will lose its magic, and then he'll lose everything that he wants at the moment.

He can't think that, though, can't let himself, not if he's going to manage to make it through the next day and a half and enjoy himself as much as possible while doing so. He pushes the thoughts to the back of his mind as he washes, scrubbing quickly so that he's done before Brendan even makes it out of bed.

The coffee is just finishing when Dylan makes it out of the bathroom, a towel wrapped around his waist and water still glistening on his torso. One very nice feature of this thing between them is that he doesn't have to try to get dressed in the bathroom for modesty's sake, which means that he doesn't have to deal with the humid air that turns the bathroom into a sauna and leaves him feeling sticky, no matter how many times he runs the towel over his skin. It's so much easier to dry off out in the main bedroom.

Plus, it's fun to watch Brendan wake up to the show he's putting on.

Dylan usually isn't nearly this flamboyant when he gets dressed, but when he sees Brendan watching him from the bed, peering out through his lashes as his hand slips down under the sheet to his cock, Dylan makes the most of the fact that he's naked, dancing around and bending over in what he hopes is a suggestive manner as he pulls things from his suitcase.

Once he shimmies into his boxers, he pauses, frowning, and sits down on the bed next to Brendan. "Hey," he says, brushing his finger across Brendan's cheek to wake him up a little more. "Are you wearing a costume today?" Part of Dylan wants to, but it's Monday, and the convention ends this afternoon, and most people don't wear costumes on Monday. Besides, he's worn all of his already, and it's not as though he has one that he's especially dying to wear again.

On the other hand, dressing in normal clothes is just one more way of admitting that the convention is almost over, and Dylan isn't sure he wants to do that, either. He'd like to hold onto this for as long as he possibly can, even if it's only until three or so this afternoon.

"Dunno. Are you?" Brendan mumbles, nuzzling against Dylan's hand as he blinks himself more awake. He clearly fell asleep again while Dylan was in the shower, and he looks so cute squinting up and blinking against the light that Dylan just wants to wrap him up in his arms and never let him go.

"That's why I was asking you," Dylan chides gently. "I can't decide. I've worn everything already, and it's a lot of effort to put on a costume, but not wearing one almost makes it feel like the con is over already, you know?"

"Yeah." Brendan stretches, pushing his hands up above his head and arching his back, and sits up. "I do."

"Yeah." Dylan sighs and slumps back against the wall. He really doesn't know what he wants to do, and it's ridiculous how much it's frustrating him.

"We could always, I dunno, make sure we go to panels or something," Brendan offers with a shrug and a smile. "I mean, I promised Tim and Matt I'd meet up with them at some point, but I could make sure you get to a panel if you're really concerned about making Dragon*Con last as long as possible."

"Would you stay there with me?" Dylan asks, assuming his most piteous expression and blinking at Brendan. "I might get lonely in the panel if you don't."

Brendan laughs, long and loud, but he agrees with a grin. "Of course I will. I wouldn't want you to get lonely," he adds, patting Dylan's cheek as he climbs out of bed.

Dylan laughs it off, but his heart soars as Brendan agrees. "So no costumes, then?"

"No costumes," Brendan confirms, heading straight to the coffee pot. He downs an entire cup as he gathers his things to shower, drinking it more quickly than it should be possible to down a hot beverage, and pours himself another cup before disappearing into the bathroom.

Dylan just shakes his head and chuckles under his breath as he pulls on his jeans and T-shirt. It's definitely going to be an interesting day.

DYLAN isn't sure if he wants to hug Kelly or throttle her. He and Brendan were happily watching the robot battles—which were *awesome* on so many levels, and a lot more fun than he had thought they'd be, though he should have realized they would be because there's nothing that isn't fun about people building robots for the sole purpose of destroying other robots and then putting them in a ring to see which one wins—when Kelly had texted him. Unthinking, he'd responded, letting her know where he was, and the next thing he knew, she and Sabrina were dragging him away, flashing apologetic grins at Brendan and promising to return Dylan in time for dinner.

He wasn't aware that he and Brendan had dinner plans, but he rather likes the idea, so he's not upset with the girls for that.

He is upset with them for just dragging him away, though. Brendan had promised that he'd be okay, and even looked slightly relieved at the idea of Dylan going off with Kelly and Sabrina— which Dylan is not thinking about, thank you very much—but he hated leaving Brendan alone. It seemed wrong; even though Brendan already had his phone out to text message his friends before Dylan had gotten three steps, and had probably made arrangements to meet up with them before he'd gotten out of the room. He's still not sure how Kelly and Sabrina managed to navigate to him so quickly. The ballroom was packed.

That's not going to stop Dylan from worrying.

"Stop it," Kelly tells him, hitting him hard on the upper arm.

Dylan is definitely leaning toward throttling her. "Stop what?"

"Brooding." She rolls her eyes as they round the corner into the Marriott and head for the escalators. "You're worrying about Brendan, I can tell."

"I left him alone in there!"

"The ballroom was packed, Dylan!" Sabrina exclaims, shaking her head. Her ponytail swishes back and forth as she does so, the blonde curls bouncing, and Dylan has to resist the urge to tug on it. "He's hardly alone!"

"You know what I mean!"

"Yeah, yeah." Kelly steps onto the escalator and twists around to glare at Dylan. "You left Brendan to fend for himself in the big, scary Robot Battle panel. Maybe the robots will turn on him! They might pick him up and throw him out of the ring!"

"Shut up." Dylan crosses his arms and glares at Kelly. "It's not funny."

"It is, a little, Dylan," Sabrina says, comforting him, patting his shoulder as the escalator descends. "You've only known the guy for a few days, and yet we've hardly seen you all con because you're spending time with him."

"I hung out with you Friday and Saturday, and we both ate lunch with you yesterday!"

"And last year, we could hardly ditch you! I think we spent less time apart last year than we have together this year!"

"Yeah, yeah." Dylan rolls his eyes and leads the way into the Dealers Room. The girls want to walk around again, but there's only one booth Dylan is interested in visiting—Tara's. He's hoping that she can help him with the project he's planning to do this afternoon, but that means explaining it to her, so he's glad Kelly and Sabrina are going to be easily distracted. He doesn't particularly want them to know what he's planning, or they won't give him the freedom to work on his project.

They'll decide either that he's crazy and keep him occupied all afternoon, or that it's an awesome idea, and they'll insist that he start right away and hover over him until it's done. He's not sure which would be worse. In the first case, he'd be left with nothing, which would suck, but it's not as though anyone will be let down if it's not done. In the second case, he'll get it done, but it won't be as good as it would have been if he'd been left alone to concentrate, which would suck more, because someone would be let down. Him.

Fortunately, the booth with the winged stuffed animals isn't far from Tara's booth, and Dylan is able to wander over to her while Kelly and Sabrina squeal and coo over the winged creatures. They're adorable—Dylan is secure enough in himself that he can admit that—but he doesn't think they deserve the hours of attention the girls seem to think they do.

He's glad for the distraction, though, and slips away silently, confident that they'll manage to find him when they've had their fill of cuteness for the day.

Tara is sitting on a stool behind her booth, dressed in exactly the same outfit she was wearing yesterday. She's one of the few people who is wearing any sort of costume at all, and seeing her makes Dylan wish he'd put on his pirate gear instead of slipping into jeans and a button-down shirt. Tara, however, doesn't seem to think so, and her eyes rake up and down Dylan's body appreciatively before she grins at him. "Nice costume."

"Thanks," he says dryly, rolling his eyes a little. "I'm cleverly disguised as a normal person, only I left the shirt that says so at home."

Tara laughs, pressing her hand to her chest. "Oh, Dylan, you'll never be a *normal* person." Her gaze glides up and down his body again. "You're far too good-looking for that."

Someday, Dylan will be able not to blush when girls tell him he's attractive. It's silly that he does—he's not at all interested in them, after all, so it doesn't matter if they're interested in him—but he can't seem to help it, and for some reason, Tara affects him more than most other girls. It might be the corset.

He looks down at the table as his cheeks flush. "I'm not sure if I should be flattered or offended."

"Flattered, Dylan," she says with a laugh. "Flattered."

"I'll, uh, try."

"Yeah, all right." She straightens as he looks up, beaming when she can finally meet his eyes again. "So what can I help you with? I'm sure you didn't stop by just to let me ogle you. Though if you did, that's okay," she adds with a laugh.

"No, sorry."

"Darn." Tara snaps her fingers and pouts for a second before perking up again. "So where's Brendan? And what can I help you with?"

"Brendan's not here." Dylan shrugs casually. "He's hanging out with his friends. I actually wanted to talk to you about something I'm working on for him. I think you might be able to help me."

"Really?" Tara's eyes light up and she leans forward, grinning widely. "What is it?"

Dylan looks over his shoulder to make sure Kelly and Sabrina are still occupied and turns back to Tara with a grin. "Well, here's the thing...."

BRENDAN is wedged between his bed and the wall when Dylan returns from spending time with Kelly and Sabrina. He's finished with the thing he was working on, miracle of all miracles. He managed to swing by the Art Show, talk to Jon, spend time with Tim and Matt, and complete his project, but he wedged himself in so that if Dylan came back before he finished he'd be able to hide the project and the fact that he was working on it. The problem is that he's now stuck, his knee caught under the bed and his shoulders wedged between it and the wall, back where the nightstand and other bed are holding it in place.

He's not sure how he managed to get in that position. He'd pushed the edge of the bed away from the wall, and he'd been working where he had enough room to move his arms freely, but somehow, in his excitement at finishing his project and his joy at how perfectly it turned out, he fell backward, got his knee jammed under the bed, and when he'd tried to sit up and free himself, he'd ended up with his shoulders jammed between the bed and the wall.

Given enough time, he's sure he can free himself, but he's only been stuck for a few minutes, and thus far, he's only managed to get himself stuck further. He hates to admit it, but he's extremely glad to see Dylan.

Gladder than he would have been otherwise, which is somewhat disturbing. He's not supposed to be this happy to see a guy he's only known for four days. Of course, the really disturbing part is that "only four days" thing. It feels like so much longer.

It feels like they've known each other forever.

Now, however, his focus is getting out from where he's wedged between the bed and the wall, and for that he needs Dylan's help. He doesn't even wait until he hears the door close—he's afraid Dylan will head straight into the bathroom or something and leave him stuck for another several minutes, and he can't stand the thought. "Dylan?"

"Yeah?" Dylan peers into the room, a frown marring his face as he looks around and fails to see Brendan. "Where are you?"

"Down here." Brendan wriggles some more, which only serves to get him stuck further, and tries to stretch out an arm. "Between the bed and the wall," he adds in a rather disgusted tone. He's blushing furiously, his face bright red, and he's already halfway regretting calling attention to his predicament. He might have been able to get out without Dylan noticing.

He also might win the Powerball this week, but he figures the chances are about equal, or would be if he'd bought a Powerball ticket, anyway.

Dylan's perplexed frown shifts up into a laugh as he turns the corner and sees Brendan. "Are you *stuck*?" he asks, his eyes widening in surprise as he looks down.

"Yes!" Brendan wiggles again, hitting his shoulder against something in the bed frame as he squirms. "Ow!"

"Are you okay?" Dylan immediately crouches down, trying to see how Brendan is stuck without getting on the bed or moving into the wedge. It's funny how he's staying completely out of it, even the wide part at the bottom, but Brendan can't find it in himself to laugh, with the metal whatever-it-is digging into his shoulder.

"No!" he snaps, shifting again in a futile attempt to stop the metal from digging into his flesh. "I'm not! I'm stuck, and the bed frame is digging into my arm, and my knee is under the bed, and I can't get out!" It comes out sounding far too much like a whining child and nothing like the mostly mature thirty-two-year-old he actually is.

Okay, so he's a thirty-two-year-old who is at a science fiction, fantasy, and pop culture convention, wearing a shirt that says "Just enough of a bastard to be worth liking," but that's not the point. Geek he might be—he admits that freely—but that doesn't mean he's a whiny brat or someone who can't function in society. It just means that he's passionate about a lot of genre-specific things, and that he gets really into them.

He is perfectly capable of both carrying on a coherent and pleasant conversation with a mundane and extracting himself from his current predicament. He just doesn't want to do either right now. He wants Dylan to rescue him and kiss his shoulder better, so that they can go off and enjoy dinner, and Brendan can give Dylan the thing he's been working on for the past few hours.

Okay, skip the kissing-his-shoulder-better part. They won't make dinner if that happens, and Brendan actually does want to make dinner. He made reservations at Avanzare, over in the Hyatt, and he doesn't want to be late.

They have time, of course. He didn't schedule their reservation until five thirty, and it's only about four fifteen now, but they both need to change, and he has to decide if he wants to give his project to Dylan before dinner, at dinner, or after dinner.

And before all that, he has to get unstuck.

Dylan steps into the wedge, eyeing the bed warily, and takes a closer look at Brendan's predicament. He even crouches down and tries to twist Brendan's knee free—as though Brendan hasn't already tried that—and when Brendan hisses in pain, he frowns at the bed. "I think I'm going to have to move it."

"Can't," Brendan says when Dylan starts pushing on the bed, trying to push it away from the wall. "The nightstand and other bed are blocking it."

"But I'm not stuck." Dylan climbs across the bed that has Brendan trapped and pushes at the one closer to the window, sliding it toward the chair. It moves easily, and he follows up by pushing the nightstand a few inches. At that point, Brendan is able to free himself, and he stands with a sigh of relief, unconsciously rubbing at his sore shoulder.

"Thanks."

"You're welcome." Dylan walks around the bed to look closely at Brendan. His hand feels far too good on Brendan's shoulder, and when he urges Brendan to sit and rest his knee for a bit, it feels far better than Brendan is willing to admit. Dylan sits down next to him and rubs at his knee, his fingers making small circles on the tender flesh. It should hurt, but it doesn't, it feels marvelous, and Brendan falls back on the bed with a moan.

"You're wonderful," he says in a husky voice that would invite sex if he weren't cranky, in pain, and on a time schedule. "Don't ever stop doing that."

Dylan just laughs, but he keeps rubbing circles and doesn't try to take Brendan up on the offer in his voice, so Brendan counts it as a definite win. "How'd you get stuck back there, anyway?"

Okay, Brendan counts it as a partial win. He doesn't really want to answer this yet, but it takes the decision about when to give Dylan his present out of his hands, so he is a little thankful. "I, uh, was hiding in case you came in early."

"Early?" Dylan's eyebrows shoot up and his eyes widen as he looks questioningly at Brendan. "I didn't have a planned time to come back. How could I be back early? And what were you hiding?"

He's tempted to say that he can't tell, because that was the whole point of hiding it, but it's done, and he's super pleased with how it turned out, and so Brendan grins and rolls over, grabbing the gift from where it's lying on the floor, newly exposed by the movement of the bed. "I, uh, was working on this." He thrusts his hand at Dylan and drops the item into his lap.

Dylan picks it up slowly, his eyes wide. The leather cord slowly unfurls as he pulls it up to reveal the thing that Brendan had been working on for the past few hours. "Did you...?"

"Make it?" Brendan nods, blushing. "Yeah. I mean, I got the cord from Jon, obviously, but the pendant is all me."

"And you made it for me?" Dylan asks in a soft voice. He's using a tone Brendan has never heard before, but the look of wonder on his face as he gazes at Brendan's creation tells him that it's awe.

The realization leaves Brendan feeling warm all over, and he grins widely as he nods. "Yeah. I, uh, wanted you to have it. As a reminder of this weekend."

"Like I'd need anything to help me remember," Dylan says in an amused voice, but he pulls the pendant up into his hand and presses it to his chest. "Thank you."

"You're welcome." Brendan rolls onto his side, prepared to say more, but before he can, Dylan climbs off the bed, still grinning stupidly, and heads back toward the door.

"Wait there," he tells Brendan, just before disappearing. Brendan can hear him digging in bags that he must have dropped upon entering the room, and he's back before Brendan has time to wonder what he's doing. "Here."

Brendan blinks as he takes the small box that Dylan thrusts at his stomach. He recognizes the boxes Tara uses to package up her stuff, and he feels a pang of guilt at the idea of Dylan buying him something, but the look on Dylan's face doesn't let him even consider pushing it back or not opening it.

Slowly, he pulls the lid off to reveal a stunning strip of leather. It's woven and braided in a way that Brendan has never seen before, the strands intricately knotted in a bold yet beautiful pattern. In the center of the bracelet is a piece of hammered-out metal topped by twisted wire—one of Tara's new pieces that he'd been admiring yesterday and had been sad to see gone today—and the clasp is one that she uses regularly, but the leather is definitely not from Tara. She's all about chains and metal. Despite how gorgeous this is, it's not her style.

It might be Dylan's, though.

"Did you make this?" Brendan asks, holding up the bracelet in awe.

"Yeah." Dylan's smile widens as he sits on the bed. "Great minds think alike, I guess. I made that this afternoon, with help from Tara, obviously. I knew I had to when I saw you admiring that piece yesterday."

"But… why?"

"Why'd you give me the necklace, Brendan?" Dylan slips the necklace over his head and lets the pendant hang against his chest.

"Because, I—" He cuts himself off, shaking his head. He can't say those words, not now, not yet. "I thought you'd like it."

"It's not something you picked up in the Dealers Room, Brendan. You *made* it."

"So?"

"So that's a little more than thinking I'd like it."

"Yeah, well…." Brendan shrugs. "Like I said, I wanted you to remember this weekend. Even if we don't ever see each other again," he adds is a quieter voice.

"I thought you wanted to."

"I do!" Brendan lifts his head to look Dylan straight in the eyes. "I meant what I said earlier about working it out and seeing what happens. I did. That doesn't mean real life won't get in the way. I wanted you to have that in case it did. That's all."

It's not really all. There's something about Dylan that makes Brendan want to do more than just try as hard as he can to get together over the course of the year and make him a pendant. He wants more than that, and it's utterly ridiculous. He can't really be feeling the way he thinks he does. Not now, not yet. Maybe if they do manage to get together over the next year he'll be able to believe it and put words to what he's feeling, but for now, Brendan isn't admitting it, no matter what.

"Oh." Dylan grins, though Brendan thinks he can detect a small amount of disappointment in his tone. "Well, I felt pretty much the same way. I never thought I'd connect with my roommate like this, man, and I wanted you to have something to remember it by, you know?"

"Yeah." Brendan forces his smile wider. "I do."

"Great. Well." Dylan wipes his hands on his pants. "So what are we doing for dinner? Kelly and Sabrina seemed to think that we have definite plans."

"I, uh, made reservations at that place in the Hyatt. Did you bring any nice clothes? Of the non-costume kind, I mean." He's only now realizing that while he can wear his Crowley suit and just be seen as possibly slightly overdressed, Dylan might already be in his nicest non-costume outfit. Brendan doesn't think that the place requires suits, but he's also sure that Dylan will seem out of place dressed as he is.

"I'm sure I can come up with something."

"Good." Brendan sits and scoots to the edge of the bed. "I'm, uh, going to shower, then."

"Yeah, okay." Dylan's voice seems flat to Brendan, but there isn't time to worry about it now. He needs to shower if they're going to make their reservation on time.

He'll worry about whatever it is once they get to the restaurant and fix it then.

DYLAN fingers the pendant as Brendan disappears into the shower and slips it back over his head as the bathroom door closes so he can examine it more closely. It's a flattened and curved piece of metal about a half-inch square wrapped in heavy-gauge wire that's twisted into an intricate pattern. The edges of the flat part are rolled and sanded, so they won't rub against Dylan's skin if he wears it under his shirt, and the wire is twisted into a complicated knot in the middle of the pendant, twisting around a brown and green swirled stone that reminds Dylan of Brendan's eyes. The entire thing is surrounded by a strand of chainmail links that give it a more rounded look and come up to fasten to the leather cord that Dylan recognizes from Jon's stand. It's a complicated twist of various shades of brown leather cord, knotted around itself in the back so that the length is completely adjustable.

The whole thing is gorgeous and was obviously made with great care, far more than anyone would put into something that was just so he'd remember the weekend.

That thought leads Dylan to think about what Brendan said and, more importantly, *how* he said it. He thinks about how Brendan ducked his head, and how his tone was a little flatter than Dylan has come to expect from him, and then he remembers how he responded, how flat his own tone was, and how he refused to tell Brendan what the bracelet was for until he knew what the necklace meant.

Then he looks around the room, notices that Brendan took the bracelet into the bathroom with him even though he'd left his clothes out here, slips the necklace back around his neck, and grins as he listens for the shower to start. He knows exactly how to fix this.

THE bracelet is missing from its spot on the counter when Brendan steps out of the shower. Immediately, he drops to the floor, ignoring the water he's dripping everywhere as he searches underneath the counter, in the trash can, and under everything that he can pick up. His heart pounds as he starts to think that he might have already lost it, and though his head says it's stupid to be upset over something he got twenty minutes ago from a guy he's known for four days, something clenches in his chest.

"Did I drop the bracelet out there?" he asks as he wraps the towel around his waist and steps out into the room. He keeps his gaze on the floor, hoping that he'll see it lying on the carpet, and he doesn't look up until he's all the way in the room.

"You didn't drop it," Dylan says. He's sitting on the corner of his bed, his legs spread, his elbows resting on his knees, and the bracelet hanging out of his right hand. The necklace Brendan gave him is still around his neck, but his smile is tight and his right knee is bouncing up and down as he looks at Brendan. "I, uh, slipped in and grabbed it."

The worry that had lifted from Brendan's chest when he saw the bracelet safe in Dylan's hands returns with crushing force. "You did?" he asks without attempting to hide the worry he's feeling. "Why?"

"Because we did this wrong." Dylan looks Brendan up and down. "You want to put on some clothes? I appreciate the view and all, but this will be easier without the distraction."

That just cements Brendan's worry. "Yeah, okay." He has to walk right past Dylan to get to his clothes. Instead of teasing like he might have been tempted to do earlier, Brendan just drops the towel and pulls on his boxers and jeans as quickly as possible. He picks it up again to dry off his hair before pulling his shirt over his head and then sits on the other bed, barefoot and still a little wet, but dressed.

"Thanks." Dylan flashes a strained smile and looks down at the bracelet as he runs it between his fingers. "I didn't mean to worry you," he says when he looks up again. "I just—" He pauses, licks his lips, runs his fingers through his hair, and looks up toward the ceiling as though there's a script up there.

"Just what?" Brendan asks when the silence starts to stretch into a second minute.

Dylan blows out a deep breath. "I just wanted to try this again, because I think we both, um. Anyway. Here." He thrusts the bracelet out toward Brendan. "I made this for you."

"Thanks?" Brendan slowly closes his fingers around it, half afraid that Dylan will take it back a second time.

"You're welcome." Dylan wipes his palms on his jeans. "Now ask me why."

They've already gone through this, and Brendan really doesn't want to hash it out again, but he can't say no to the pleading look on Dylan's face, so he humors him. "Okay. Why?"

"Because I want you to have something to remember the weekend. No." He shakes his head. "To remember me. I like you. A lot. And I know we said we weren't going to worry about what happens after we leave Dragon*Con, but sometimes the best-laid plans go awry once reality hits, and if that happens, I want you to know that I do want this to be more than just a weekend thing."

"Oh." Brendan rubs at the back of his neck, his face flushing as he stares down at the intricately braided leather. He's not ready to say too much about his feelings for Dylan beyond what he already has, but he can't just ignore a confession like that either. "I do too," he settles for as he lifts his gaze to look Dylan in the eyes for the first time since this conversation started. "I don't know what's going to happen once we get back to the real world, and I don't want to put a name to any of this—it's way too soon—but that's basically why I gave you the necklace."

Dylan grins. "I thought so." He moves to sit next to Brendan and takes his hand. "Let's not beat around the bush about that next time, okay? Either of us."

That was really the kind of awkward confession that only gets made once in a relationship, but Brendan agrees anyway. There will be other awkward confessions to come if this goes anywhere. That's the nature of relationships. "Okay," he says, and manages to suppress his chuckle, though he can't keep the corners of his mouth from turning up into a grin. "No more beating around the bush when it comes to not naming the things we're feeling. Got it."

Dylan snorts. "Yeah, that, exactly. Thanks. I feel so much better now."

"Good." Brendan slips the bracelet around his wrist and grins when it fits perfectly. "Shall we go to dinner now?" He needs to change his shirt, as does Dylan, but they still have a little bit of time before they need to be at the restaurant.

"We could." Dylan doesn't sound too interested. "Or, I was thinking, maybe we could go use the pool and then order room service instead? It's usually pretty empty right about now, and, I don't know. I'm not really in the mood for a stuffy dinner."

Brendan actually likes nice dinners and doesn't usually take showers before he swims, but he likes the idea of getting Dylan into a swimsuit as well and seeing him all wet and half naked. He can imagine the pool water dripping off Dylan's chest, droplets rolling over his muscles, outlining the curves and planes of his chest and....

He shakes his head, clearing it of that image. The real thing is right here and better, even if he is currently clothed and dry. He isn't going to pass up the opportunity to see that outside of his imagination, though. "Yeah. Sure. Let me just call and cancel our reservation."

THE pool is awesome, just as Dylan knew it would be, but it's even more fun than he expected. Swimming with Brendan is infinitely preferable to swimming with Eric, who has always dragged Dylan to the pool in years past because he thinks he'll get hot babes by parading around in his swim trunks. It also carries with it perks that Dylan never would have thought about had he not insisted that they skip their dinner reservations in favor of hitting the pool. Most of the advantages come in the form of not being in constant danger of being splashed or dunked, Eric's favorite activities, but Dylan manages to steal a few kisses, too, pulling Brendan close without regard to who's around, and that's the best part of all.

They stay for close to two hours, alternating between the big pool and the hot tub until Brendan is shivering and Dylan is burning up and neither of them want to spend another minute in the water, or at least not chlorinated water in a public place. Dylan definitely has plans for when they get to the shower.

First, though, he has to warm Brendan up, so he comes up behind him, wrapping both a towel and his arms around him, and guides him over to the side of the pool deck, where they stand, gazing out the windows at the street a few stories below.

The vendors are leaving, and the parking lot across the street from the Marriott is full of people loading vans and trucks with unsold merchandise. Dylan sees several things he would have bought had his funds and packing space been unlimited, and he points one of them out to Brendan, sighing wistfully as he watches the coveted items disappearing into the vehicle.

"Yeah," Brendan agrees, sighing as well. "The latex weapons guys are loading over there." He points toward another van. "Man, would I like to own a few of those."

"You boffer LARP?" The idea of Brendan participating in actual combat with padded foam weapons known as boffers adds a whole new dimension to the idea of him dressing up in costume for a Live Action Role Playing game. Dylan likes it.

"Not often." Brendan leans his head back against Dylan's shoulder. "Mostly I just think they look cool. I would have *loved* to have one as a kid, you know? I wouldn't have gotten in trouble for hitting Alex or Melanie with that."

Dylan thinks about how his parents would have reacted to him coming after Jake or Katrina with a latex foam sword and raises his eyebrows. "Really?"

"Well, not as much trouble as I did when I hit Mel with the wooden sword I got. At least the latex ones are *designed* for hitting people. Apparently wooden swords aren't. They hurt too much."

"Huh." Dylan twists his head to gaze down at Brendan. "I thought swords were intended to hurt people."

"Well, yeah, but apparently younger siblings do not qualify as an invading army or a suitable practice companion for a knight in training, so hitting them is a big no-no. At least," he adds, sighing dramatically, "that's what my parents told me."

"What's their position on older siblings? Do *they* qualify as an invading army or suitable practice companion?"

"You know? I never asked." Brendan shakes his head. "The idea of hitting Alex with it never occurred to me, probably because I knew he'd get me back somehow, even if he didn't get to hit me himself. Mel was a safe target. Alex was dangerous."

"The perils of being a middle child."

"Right?" Brendan grins as he relaxes more, leaning heavily on Dylan's chest with his head once more on Dylan's shoulder. He turns it to the side a little to grin at Dylan. "I was six when Mel was born, and, man, did I hate suddenly being the middle child. The baby gets all the benefits, you know?"

"Yeah." Dylan nods fervently. Katrina definitely got more of just about everything than Dylan had while growing up, though he'd never felt unloved or neglected, really. He just hadn't been able to get away with as much. Of course, Katrina wielded a mean set of puppy-dog eyes, better than either Jacob or Dylan could manage, and that might have had something to do with it too.

Maybe.

"It sucked, man, and I'm pretty sure that it was even worse since Mel was a girl. I think Momma always wanted one, and once she had Mel, she doted on her. Everyone did."

"You're not jealous of your baby sister, are you, Brendan?"

"Of course not." Brendan turns around in Dylan's arms, looping his hands around Dylan's neck and gazing straight into his eyes. "She doesn't have anyone like you."

It's sickeningly sweet and sappy, the kind of thing that should make Dylan run for the hills, but instead it leaves him feeling warm inside, full of happiness, pride, and something that he's still not quite willing to put a name to, and he smiles widely before leaning down and kissing Brendan soundly.

When he pulls back, he's wearing a ridiculously wide grin, and he feels like his heart is going to beat its way out of his chest, it's pounding so hard. He has to infuse a little bit of humor into the situation, or he's going to end up squealing like a little girl. "So you're really planning on keeping me, then?"

"As long as I can manage it."

It's a good thing that they're the only ones on the pool deck right then, because Dylan feels like he's going to explode with joy, and he's grinning so widely he's sure that his face is going to split in two. There's so much he wants to say to that, so many questions he wants to ask, but he doesn't want to ruin the moment, so instead he pulls Brendan in for another kiss, pressing their bodies together as he slips his tongue into Brendan's mouth and forgets about everything else as he loses himself in the sensation.

BRENDAN grins widely as Dylan crawls back up the bed. "Everything taken care of?"

"Tray's out in the hallway. Do not disturb sign is on the door." Dylan reaches over and presses a button on his cell phone. "Phone is off. I'm all yours."

"Good." Brendan reaches over and makes sure his own phone is off before dropping it on the nightstand and pushing Dylan down on the bed. "That's what I like to hear." He lets his gaze travel down Dylan's body, grinning when he sees that Dylan didn't take off his boxers after putting the tray of food out in the hallway. He can work with this. "Lift your hips."

Dylan's eyes grow dark with desire as he complies, and his cock springs free, already half erect, as Brendan slides the black satin over the curve of Dylan's ass and down his long legs. They move easily, the satin slipping over Dylan's skin with more ease than cotton, but Brendan secretly misses Dylan's character-imprinted cotton boxers. These feel like Dylan is trying to impress him, which is nice but unnecessary. He's way past impressed now, and the idea that Dylan is trying to make himself look good is equally endearing and amusing.

He tosses the boxers behind him, not paying attention to where they land, and slides his hands back up Dylan's legs, pushing them apart so he can kneel between them as he leans forward to lick along the length of Dylan's cock. Dylan gasps, his hips bucking, and Brendan opens his mouth, letting Dylan push himself inside before pulling back to swirl his tongue over the tip, tasting the salty precome as he sucks and licks.

Dylan moans, his fingers clenching in the sheets. His muscles are taut as Brendan slides his hands up over his hips to his stomach and then back down, caressing along the inside of Dylan's legs before slipping one hand down to fondle his balls. It's almost obscene, the way Dylan is moaning, his head tipped back to expose the long column of his throat and his whole body trembling with the effort of staying still.

Brendan puts his hands on Dylan's hips, steadying him before he opens his mouth wider, sliding it all the way down Dylan's cock, and hollows his cheeks as he sucks. He slides back slowly, humming and sucking as he moves and swirls his tongue over the tip again before sliding back down. Dylan writhes and bucks, moaning out Brendan's name even as Brendan takes him deeper, one hand returning to fondle his balls as he opens his throat and slides his lips down to the base of Dylan's cock once more.

"God! Brendan!" Dylan's hips thrust forward, almost gagging Brendan, but the sounds he's making as he writhes makes the minor discomfort worth it.

Giving blow jobs to Dylan is nothing like giving blow jobs to anyone else has ever been. Brendan has always prided himself at being good at them and has always made sure that he gives at least as many as he receives, but with Dylan, it's different. He wants this to be more than good, he wants it to be incredible, he wants to lick and suck until Dylan calls out his name as he comes and is left boneless on the bed, spent just from the power of Brendan's lips and tongue.

This is about more than reciprocating the admittedly phenomenal blow job he got while they showered together after returning from the pool. This is about making Dylan feel unbelievable, and about how wonderful it makes Brendan feel to make him come undone. This is about giving truly feeling better than receiving, and about the way that Brendan's heart beats faster with every moan of pleasure that escapes Dylan's lips.

Brendan is hard just from the noises Dylan is making, hovering on the edge even as he teases Dylan closer and closer to it, and when Dylan's hips buck that final time, and he comes, spilling into Brendan's mouth as he calls out Brendan's name, Brendan comes, too, opening his mouth in a moan of pleasure as his whole body shudders.

He collapses on top of Dylan when he's done, his head resting on Dylan's belly and his body sprawled on the wet mess between Dylan's legs. It's uncomfortable and mildly disgusting, but he's too spent to even contemplate moving, not even to get out of the wet spot. Dylan's hands wrap around his shoulders, pulling him up so his head is on Dylan's chest, and he sighs, letting his eyes drift closed as he relaxes against Dylan.

"Are you falling asleep on me?" Dylan asks in an amused tone after a minute passes without either of them moving at all.

"Maybe." Brendan manages to snuggle a little closer, but he doesn't open his eyes. He's too content to have any desire to move at all.

"We should move to the other bed. And clean off so we don't have to shower again."

"Ugh." Brendan lifts his head and scowls. He hates the idea of moving, but he hates the idea of waking up with dried come all over his lower body even more, and if he's going to have to shower in the morning—which he really doesn't want to do, especially since he took two showers tonight already—he's going to have to get up even earlier. "You go get the washcloth."

"Yes, sir!" Dylan mock salutes as he eases them both into an upright position. "Get on the other bed. I'm not sleeping in the wet spot tonight."

Brendan scoops his boxers from the floor as he moves across the aisle between the beds. He drops them onto the covers and sits on the edge to wait for Dylan, careful not to get any of the white fluid that's coating his stomach and groin onto the still-clean sheets. While he's waiting, he pulls his cell phone over from the nightstand. He has to call and make sure he's going to be able to catch a shuttle back to the airport so he's not stuck taking MARTA with luggage again. He's just turning on the phone when Dylan returns, drops the washcloth into his lap, and takes the phone from his hands.

"I thought we agreed no phones tonight."

"We did, but I haven't called to arrange my ride for tomorrow yet." Brendan wipes himself off and returns the washcloth to Dylan, who tosses it onto the other bed. "I have to make sure I can get a shuttle to take me back to the airport." He needs to pack, too, but as Dylan pulls him down into bed, he decides that can wait until morning, even if it means that he needs to get up a little earlier. "I need to know what time it's coming so I can schedule a wake-up call. You might be driving," he adds as he cuddles up next to Dylan, "but I have a plane to catch."

"Skip it."

Brendan lifts his head to stare incredulously at Dylan. "*Skip it*? Dylan, I can't just *skip* my flight! How would I get home?"

Dylan sucks his bottom lip into his mouth, his whole body stilling as he looks up at Brendan through lowered lashes. "Ride with me?"

"Ride with you?" Brendan repeats, dumbly. "Dylan, Buffalo and Albany aren't exactly right next to each other. I can't ask you to drive me! Besides, I've already paid for my plane ticket."

"You weren't asking. I was offering. And it's not really that far out of my way," Dylan lifts his head to look earnestly at Brendan.

"It's a completely different route, because I'd take 75 to 71 and across Ohio and Pennsylvania to Buffalo and then take 90 East to Albany instead of taking 85 to 81, but it only adds about three hours to my drive time. I looked it up this afternoon."

"But you stop halfway, don't you?" Brendan can't believe he's even thinking about this, and yet he can't stop. The idea of having another day with Dylan is tempting, too tempting, and his heart is fluttering at the idea that Dylan looked up the drive times just to see if he could make the offer.

"Yeah, but it's not like I have reservations or anything. I just pull off at a Motel 6 or whatever. All I need is a clean bed to crash in for the night."

"I can't." Brendan sighs. "I want to, I do, but I'm going back to work on Thursday. I need a day off to recover from the con, and do laundry, and take care of all those little real-life things that are waiting for me at home. If I don't get back until Wednesday afternoon, I won't get most of it done, and I'll be too tired to be effective at work on Thursday."

"Call out?" Dylan's tone is hopeful, but his eyes tell Brendan he already knows what the answer to that is. Brendan can't, no matter how much he wants to, not with everything he has waiting back at work for him. He's a copy editor and works from home a lot, but he wouldn't be able to access his e-mail from the road, and it's close enough to press time for one of their major magazines that there will be plenty he needs to look at.

"I *wish*," Brendan said ruefully, shaking his head. "I can't, though. Really. I'm going to have too much to do as it is."

"And will one more day make that much of a difference?"

The hope in Dylan's voice is almost Brendan's undoing, but he has to stay strong in this instance. His boss won't appreciate him returning later than planned, and he really needs to save both his vacation days and his boss's goodwill if he wants to sneak away later in the year to visit Dylan. "Not really, but it'll mean one less day I'll have later to come visit you. And I've already paid for my plane ticket. It's nonrefundable."

"You were going to come visit me?"

"Well, I was hoping to. If you want me to, and I can get the days off work."

"Of course I want you to." Dylan squeezes Brendan tightly. "I just didn't think you would."

"Why wouldn't I? I said I wanted to do what I could to make this work, didn't I? That means we're going to have to visit each other, you know."

Dylan's smile is blinding. "Yeah, I know. I just, I don't know, didn't really think too much about the logistics of it."

"Of course you didn't." Brendan says it fondly. He knows he hasn't known Dylan that long and really can't know him all that well, but he's confident that he's correct in the assessment that Dylan just decides things need to happen and worries about the logistics later. He probably gets almost everything accomplished, too, without planning ahead of time, whereas Brendan plans everything out as much as possible. He's sure it's one of the reasons Dylan was so stressed on Thursday—he'd planned and then it hadn't worked out.

Dylan opens his mouth to protest, but Brendan stops him with a kiss, and when they break apart, Dylan is grinning. "At least let me drive you to the airport, then."

"You don't have to."

Dylan reaches up and cups Brendan's chin, forcing him to look straight into Dylan's eyes. "I want to," he says in a slow, firm voice before pulling Brendan down for another kiss. "What time's your flight?"

"A little after noon, so I need to be at the airport around eleven."

"So if we leave here by nine thirty, we can take MARTA to get my car, check out, and get you to the airport on time. And I'll actually hit the road at a decent hour."

That does sound appealing. It will probably let Brendan get up later than he would have had to if he were catching the shuttle, and even if it doesn't, it means extra time with Dylan, which he is definitely in favor of. "You sure?"

"Duh." Dylan's grin widens as he looks back at Brendan. "Wouldn't have offered if I didn't. Gives us more time before we have to say good-bye, and you don't have to worry about taking your luggage on the train again."

Brendan rolls his eyes. Okay, so he might have gotten a little irritable about that on Thursday. Sue him. He had been a little stressed out then, and exiting the station at the wrong place hadn't helped at all. It's not as though he's afraid to take MARTA again or anything like that. He can't actually say that, though, so he just leans down and presses a quick kiss to Dylan's lips before resting his head on Dylan's shoulder again. "Sounds good. You set the alarm?"

Dylan reaches over and picks up the phone, somehow managing to dial the correct number without dislodging Brendan. "Eight work for you?" When Brendan nods, he puts in the request, hangs up the phone, and sighs as he wraps his arms back around Brendan.

Brendan reaches over him and turns out the bedside lamp, plunging the room into darkness. "Night," he whispers, pressing his body as close to Dylan's as possible before letting his muscles relax and giving into the weariness that's threatening to overcome him.

"Night," Dylan replies, kissing the top of Brendan's head and lying back with a sigh. He relaxes under Brendan quickly, his breathing evening out before Brendan drifts off, and it's this moment that Brendan is going to remember until he has the opportunity to fall asleep on Dylan again.

The moment is perfect, and if Brendan could bottle it and keep it forever, he would.

SAUNTERING VAGUELY DOWNWARD

TUESDAY

MORNING comes far too early. Morning always comes far too early the Tuesday after Dragon*Con is over, as far as Dylan is concerned, but this Tuesday seems to come especially early. When the phone rings at eight, waking Dylan up, the first and only thought that runs through his head is that he only has three more hours with Brendan, and then he won't see him again for weeks at least, probably months or even a year, if ever. It's entirely possible that, despite what they both want, they'll manage to drift apart before they meet up again, and that they'll completely miss each other—or avoid each other—at next year's convention.

There's nothing to do but make the best of it, though, so when Dylan puts the phone back on the hook, he strokes his fingers lightly along Brendan's cheek. "Hey," he says when Brendan's eyes flutter open. "Time to get up."

"Already?" Brendan stretches one arm up into the air, and when he lowers it, Dylan catches his hand and brings it to his lips.

"Yeah. Already." His lips curve up into a melancholy smile. "We gotta get packed so we can head over to pick up my car."

"I'd rather just stay here." Brendan rolls onto his back, pulling Dylan with him so their positions are reversed and Dylan is looking down at Brendan's sleepy smile. "I'm comfortable."

"You don't want to miss your flight, remember?" There's a big part of Dylan that's tempted to just give in and lie in bed until they're ready to get up. If Brendan misses his flight, then he'll have no choice but to ride with Dylan, and they'll have an extra day together. He can't, though, not after what Brendan told him last night. Getting Brendan to ride with him might be a surer bet than getting Brendan to visit him, but he likes the second idea a lot more, and he wants to hold onto the hope of it happening.

"Yeah, yeah." Brendan pulls Dylan down for a brief kiss, pecking him on the lips before pulling back and smiling sadly. "Let's go."

Dylan can't let that be the last kiss they have in bed together. He leans down, capturing Brendan's lips in a kiss that leaves his heart pounding and his head spinning. He puts every bit of emotion he's feeling into it, his desire to stay with Brendan, his melancholy at the thought of being separated, his joy that the weekend turned out so much better than he could possibly have anticipated, and that undefined passion that he won't put a name to until he meets with Brendan again, outside of Dragon*Con.

Brendan reciprocates, pouring passion and desire into the kiss and leaving Dylan reeling. They're both grinning widely when they pull back, and Dylan leans down, resting his forehead against Brendan's. "Good morning."

"Now it is," Brendan agrees, rolling them back over and pressing another quick kiss to Dylan's lips before climbing off him, sitting up and stretching in one smooth movement.

Watching Brendan's muscles flex as he stretches and climbs from the bed, Dylan can't help but agree. No matter what the rest of the morning brings, it's definitely off to a very good start.

MARTA is much more fun to ride with someone, Brendan decides as the train pulls out of Peachtree Center Station, heading toward Lennox and Dylan's car. Of course, Brendan is convinced that doing anything with Dylan, even the most unpleasant tasks, would be enjoyable, simply because it means that he gets to do them with Dylan, and that means spending time with him. It's ridiculous how enjoyable packing up was—grown men are not supposed to find pleasure in throwing clothing and bedding at each other from across the room—and Dylan even managed to make an adventure out of picking breakfast at the Caribou Coffee in the food court before heading down to the MARTA station. Brendan has never heard so many ridiculous descriptions of pastries and coffees, and he was almost positive that he wasn't going to be able to eat anything at all, until he realized that Dylan was skillfully persuading him to pick the sweetest, most sugary thing on the menu.

On a normal day, Brendan would have protested and just not eaten to prove a point. Today, he gave in with a smile and ended up with a chocolate concoction that tasted surprisingly good. He's rather irritated by that—he didn't want to like it—but at the same time, he's glad he let Dylan persuade him. It's one last crazy thing to do at Dragon*Con before he parts ways with Dylan for the next several weeks.

He's not going to think about the possibility of it being longer.

Instead, he reaches over, puts his hand on Dylan's knee, and squeezes to get his attention. "Do you know how to get back to the hotel from the station?"

"Yeah." Dylan laughs. "Back is easy. It's right near the highway and you get on after the toll portion ends, so there's no huge detour to miss that. Getting there's what's hard, unless you want to pay a toll, which I am so doing next year. If I hadn't had GPS, I would have been totally lost getting there, 'cause I told it I didn't want to get on the toll road. It took me on this ridiculous detour through the city that I don't think I could duplicate without the GPS if you paid me."

"I doubt anyone would be willing to pay you for that," Brendan tells him dryly, though his lips curve up into a smile. "Unless you're planning on moving to Atlanta and becoming a bus or taxi driver, it's probably pretty useless knowledge as far as making money goes."

"Well, darn." Dylan snaps his fingers. "Guess I'll have to find another get-rich-quick plan."

Brendan laughs. "Let me know if you figure it out."

"Who says I'm going to share the knowledge?"

"Me." He leans in and kisses Dylan gently on the lips. "It's in your best interest to do so, you know."

"Is it now?"

"Yep." Brendan grins as he pulls back. "It is. If we both get rich quickly, then we can quit our jobs, move somewhere together, and spend all day every day lounging in bed having sex."

"Oh really?" Dylan's eyes are glittering with amusement. "And what makes you think that I want to lounge in bed all day having sex with you?"

"Well," Brendan drawls, sliding his hand up Dylan's thigh, "there were a few things you said earlier." He squeezes briefly and slides his hand over, brushing it across Dylan's groin before pulling it back to his lap. "But if you don't want to...." He shrugs, grinning wickedly. "It was just a suggestion."

Dylan jostles his shoulder. "I hate you."

"Yeah, I can tell. I mean, the whole asking me to ride back to New York with you was a big clue. So was how you kissed me earlier. I mean, man, *that* was torture."

"Yep. Things I do to everyone I hate. I would never subject someone I liked to that."

"Obviously. It was pure agony." Brendan manages a smile and concentrates on letting the banter distract him. They're almost to Lennox Station now, and all he can think about is that they'll disembark there, and then all that's left is the trip back to the hotel and the trip to the airport. He's not sure he's ready for that.

DYLAN watches the bellhop load the last of their bags onto the cart and immediately turns around and drops to his knees so he can check under the beds and chairs one last time. He hears Brendan chuckle behind him as he shoves his head under the first bed, but he ignores it, shuffling over to the second bed once he's determined—again—that the first is clear. "I'm looking for your stuff too, you know," he calls over his shoulder as he scoots across the aisle. "You shouldn't laugh."

Brendan comes up behind him and leans down, resting his hand on Dylan's shoulder. "You're not going to find anything."

He's right—this is the fourth time Dylan has checked since they finished packing—but he can't stop himself from looking again, just to be sure. Every time he checks out of a hotel, Dylan has this nagging feeling that he's leaving something important behind, and it's even worse than usual today. Looking is the only thing that makes him feel even a little bit better, even though he knows he's not going to find anything, and he has a sneaking suspicion as to why he feels like he's leaving something behind.

In under an hour, when he drops Brendan off at the airport, he will be.

The knowledge doesn't help him shake the feeling, though, so he checks under the desk and chairs and in the bathroom again before he takes Brendan's hand and they follow the bellhop from the room. As the door clicks shut, Dylan twitches, fighting down the urge to pull his keycard from his pocket and dash back inside to check yet again.

Brendan laughs as he tugs Dylan down the hall after the bellhop. "We have everything, I promise. You checked four times, and I checked before that. There's nothing to worry about."

Dylan nods. He knows this, he does, and he knows it's just this silly feeling that he can't shake, but the knowledge doesn't help much. He's trying to calm down, sucking in deep breaths and releasing them slowly, when another thought occurs to him and he stops in the middle of the hallway, turning to look at Brendan with wide eyes. "The safe! Did we get everything out of the safe?"

"Yes, Dylan." Somehow, despite the fact that this is the first time they've checked out of a hotel room together, Brendan manages to sound as though he's answered this question countless times on countless vacations.

It's a nice thought that Brendan might keep sounding like this year after year, and Dylan can't help but grin through his nervousness. "Are you sure?"

"Yes." Brendan starts walking again, pulling Dylan with him as they hurry to catch up to the bellhop. "Our laptops were in there, remember? We got everything out when we packed them up."

"What about the desk drawers?" There are so many places things could get hidden in a hotel room, and Dylan is sure he didn't check them all. "Or the nightstand drawers?"

"Did you put anything in either of them?"

"No, but—"

"Then there's nothing in them." Brendan stops when they reach the elevator bay, turning to take both of Dylan's hands in his and looking him straight in the eyes. "You didn't put anything in them. I didn't put anything in them. That means there's nothing in them. I promise, our stuff didn't grow legs while we weren't looking and hide from us."

"But—" Dylan isn't even sure why he's protesting now. He just feels like he has to.

Brendan tugs on his hands, pulling him closer and cutting him off. "Dylan. Seriously, man. Relax. We have everything. We're going to go downstairs, check out, load the car, and we'll be on our way before you know it. *With* all our stuff."

That's the problem. They will be on the road before he knows it, and Dylan doesn't want to be. He never wants to leave Dragon*Con on Tuesday, and he always wishes that it would go on longer, but this year, he's even less ready to depart than usual. He doesn't want to leave Brendan. "I know, but—"

"But nothing." Brendan pulls Dylan in and kisses him tenderly. "Take a deep breath and try to stop thinking about it. It will all work out. I promise."

Dylan wants to believe that. He wants to believe that he'll see Brendan again in a few weeks, a couple of months at most, and that next year, they'll be rooming together again, and not by accident this time. Next year they'll plan to room together, they'll travel together, and there won't be any question about seeing each other again in the future.

He has to believe that.

Taking another deep breath, Dylan manages a nod and a smile that grows when Brendan returns it. "Yeah, okay." He leans in, kisses Brendan yet again, and steps onto the elevator.

He's going to make this work.

A DISAPPOINTINGLY short amount of time later, Dylan carefully maneuvers his car through the twisting roads of Hartsfield-Jackson Atlanta International Airport. He hates driving in airports, hates trying to figure out which lane he needs to be in to get to the right terminal, and when it's okay to cut around the stopped shuttle, or when it will leave him in the wrong lane with no time to get over to where he needs to be. He always feels like he has to concentrate extra hard just to get to the passenger pick-up and drop-off area, and today it's even more difficult.

He doesn't want to pay attention to the road. He wants to pay attention to the guy in the passenger seat. He likes having Brendan ride with him.

Even the relatively short trip from the Marriott unloading circle to the airport has been far more pleasant than the trips he's used to taking. Usually, when he's driving, he has either Eric or Katrina in the passenger seat, and neither is as pleasant or entertaining as Brendan is. In Katrina's defense, she's usually deliberately not entertaining—that's what little sisters are for, after all—and she has gotten better since graduating from college. They have an almost pleasant relationship now, but Dylan still doesn't think that she could keep him as entertained as Brendan has, even on a trip this short. Eric could keep him entertained—he's done so on the long trip from New York before—but he's Eric. Dylan loves his best friend like a brother, but he's a little rough around the edges and entertaining in a completely different way than Brendan is.

While Eric would have cracked jokes and laughed at some of the crazy vehicles they've passed or been passed by, Brendan has kept up a steady flow of intelligent and interesting conversation. It's a nice change, and one that's going to make the silence of the trip on the way home seem painful, instead of the relief it was on the way up. Dylan had enjoyed the novelty of driving by himself on the way to Dragon*Con, but he's sure that he's going to find the trip home long and lonely.

In a way, he's almost glad for the complicated airport roads. They demand his full attention, keeping his mind off everything that's about to happen. He focuses on the roads, lets Brendan's soft, melodious voice wash over him, and tries to just stay in the moment. Even with cars whose drivers know where they're going zooming around him and the airport signs that seem to be telling him to go in five different directions at once, this is good.

It's going to be a little less good in just a minute, though. The signs have finally led him somewhere, and the passenger drop-off area is just ahead. Within a minute, he'll be at his destination. Or at least, at Brendan's destination.

Dylan lets the car coast to a stop in the passenger drop-off area, puts it in park, and twists in his seat to look at Brendan. "So. Here you are."

"Here I am." Brendan wipes his hands on his jeans and gives Dylan a wan smile. "Thanks for the ride."

"Sure. You, uh, you have everything?"

"In the trunk."

"Right." Dylan barely resists the urge to smack his forehead. "Um, let me, uh, let me help you get that."

"I can—"

"No, I'll, uh, yeah." He climbs from the car before he can say anything else, hoping that maybe the dubiously fresh air of the passenger drop-off area will clear his head and remind him that he is perfectly capable of coherent conversation, thank you very much, even when it's conversation that he doesn't particularly want to have.

Brendan climbs out of the car too, and when he slams the door shut, the sound resonates through Dylan's bones, sending a shiver down his spine. He disguises it by jerking the trunk lid open, and by the time Brendan joins him, he's already pulled Brendan's backpack and checked bag out. "Here," he says, handing over the backpack as Brendan reaches for the laptop.

"Thanks." Brendan sets the backpack down on the edge of the trunk, letting it lean against his stomach as he slips the laptop strap over his shoulder.

"You're welcome." Dylan manages a small smile and claps Brendan firmly on the shoulder. He's afraid to do more, afraid that if he gives into the urge to hug and kiss Brendan, he won't actually let him leave. "So, uh, call or text when you land?"

"Of course." The smile Brendan flashes looks as strained as Dylan's feels, and when his hand comes up to Dylan's shoulder, Dylan can't take it anymore.

"You'd better," he says, sliding his hand along the back of Brendan's neck and pulling him in for a tight hug. He lets his hands slide down Brendan's back, slipping them under the strap of the laptop bag, and squeezes as hard as he can, holding Brendan close and breathing in his scent as he buries his face in the join of his neck and shoulder.

It only takes Brendan about five seconds to respond, letting the laptop bag fall heavily against their sides as he wraps himself around Dylan, his hands sliding under Dylan's shirt as he presses himself so close that Dylan almost thinks he's trying to permanently attach himself.

Not that Dylan would have any issue with that idea. If Brendan was permanently attached, he wouldn't have to say good-bye right now. At the moment, he's willing to deal with the whole host of other problems it would present, just to avoid that.

When they finally pull apart, there are definitely not tears in Dylan's eyes. They're watering a little, but that's just all the carbon monoxide in the air from the idling vehicles, including his, and has nothing to do with saying good-bye to Brendan. Nothing at all. He's a grown man, and he can handle this, whatever happens. He can have faith.

"So, um, have a good flight. I guess," he says, wiping surreptitiously at his eyes as Brendan swings the backpack onto his back.

"Yeah. Drive safe." Brendan hesitates for a moment before he reaches up, grabs the front of Dylan's shirt, and pulls him down for a kiss. It's awkward at first, with Dylan's hands flailing out as he tries to catch his balance, and their lips more mashing together than moving with each other, but when Dylan gets his balance back under control and Brendan tilts his head just a little to the right, it's wonderful. When Brendan slips his tongue between Dylan's lips, lightly teasing as he slides it around Dylan's, it's perfect.

This time when they break apart, Dylan is grinning. "I'll see you," he whispers as he rests his forehead against Brendan's.

"You will," Brendan promises, a small smile gracing his lips as he leans up and presses them chastely to Dylan's one last time.

"You're not getting rid of me that easily. And I'm sure I'm not going to be able to ditch you."

"True." Dylan pulls the retractable handle on Brendan's luggage out and presses it into his hand, wrapping his hand around Brendan's and squeezing it before drawing back. He lets his fingers linger as long as possible on Brendan's skin, keeping contact while Brendan grabs his guitar from the trunk, and then he forces a smile on his face, pats Brendan on the shoulder, and turns back to the car.

He watches over the roof as Brendan walks inside, his eyes staying on Brendan's retreating figure until it's lost behind the sliding doors and the masses of bodies going through them. When he's certain he can't see Brendan anymore, Dylan climbs into the car and carefully maneuvers his way back into traffic.

It's going to be a long drive home.

BRENDAN manages to keep his head held high as he checks in his luggage, makes his way through security, and finds his gate. It's not until he's waiting in the boarding area with forty minutes to kill and nothing to do but think about the weekend that he slumps down, his eyes closing as he lets his head fall back against the chair he's sitting in.

It's awkward and uncomfortable, and if he stays like this for long he's not going to be able to get up to board the plane, much less sit through the entire flight, but it's distracting. Focusing on the physical pain is easier than focusing on the emotional pain that he knows he'll feel if he just gives into it.

It's stupid. He hasn't even known Dylan for five full days, and yet he feels like there's this hollow place inside him, and has ever since he walked away from the car. It was a great weekend, sure, but Brendan has had great weekends before, both at Dragon*Con and elsewhere, and none of them have left him feeling like this. None of them have left him wanting to pursue things further and see exactly where they can go.

Something is different about this time, and that's as scary as it is exhilarating.

He can't let himself think about it, though, not if he wants to stay sane long enough to get home and set plans for visiting Albany in motion, so he pulls his backpack closer and starts digging for a book to keep him occupied. He falters momentarily when his fingers brush over *Stardust* and he remembers that brief conversation from Friday morning where he offered to lend it to Dylan, but he pushes the thought aside and pulls out his battered copy of *Good Omens* instead. That makes him think of Dylan too, and the ridiculous argument they had about it, but it doesn't carry with it the regret of not lending it out, and Brendan finds it easy to get absorbed in the book.

When he reads it, time passes quickly, and if his luck holds, he'll be on the plane and heading home before he has too much time to think about anything.

Once he's there, that's when the real challenge will begin.

EPILOGUE

DYLAN ROJERS bounces on his toes as he looks down over the railing onto the lobby level of the Atlanta Marriott Marquis. Behind him, the Pulse Lounge is filling up, eager geeks mingling with people in town for other events. Below, the overworked bellhops are pulling carts filled with the most interesting things. Dylan is having great fun trying to see if he can spot what someone will be dressing as from the bits and pieces that stick out of their luggage, and every time he makes a connection, his grin grows wider.

The 501st is out in force this year—there are currently four carts carrying stormtrooper armor and helmets sitting in the lobby—and the usual wings, lightsabers, and swords are present as well. There are two bulky items on one cart that Dylan can't identify, however, and he nudges Eric's shoulder and points excitedly. "What do you think those are?"

"No clue." Eric leans forward, his arms resting on top of the rail and his forehead resting on his arms. "And I don't care, either."

Dylan's mouth drops open in surprise. "Dude. What crawled up your butt and died?"

Eric straightens with a sigh. "Nothing. I'm just bored, and I don't understand why we're standing here watching people *check in* when there's a bar less than thirty feet away."

"Because it's two fifteen on a Thursday afternoon?" Dylan offers, frowning at his friend. "What's wrong, man? Seriously. You used to love doing this."

"You used to be more interested in what people had on their carts than who was walking through the door."

Dylan can't deny that. He's been perking up every time a relatively tall, dark-haired guy walks into the lobby, hoping that it's the person he's waiting for. So far, it hasn't been. "Touché."

"So excuse me for not being overly enthusiastic about standing here waiting for your boyfriend." Eric rolls his eyes. "He has your phone number, you know, and you have his. He'll call when he gets here, or you could text him and say we'll be in the bar."

Brendan would and Dylan could, but that's not what he wants. "I want to meet him downstairs. Like last year." Only this year, he plans on it being a much more pleasant experience.

"You're both already checked into your room!" Eric throws up his hands and sighs dramatically when Dylan sets his lips and crosses his arms. "Fine. We'll watch from here. You're pathetic, you know that?"

"Am not!" Only, he is, and he knows it. It's something Dylan has come to accept over the past year, though he'll never admit it, especially not to Eric.

"Are too." Eric twists around, leaning with his back against the railing and shakes his head at Dylan. "Beyond pathetic, man."

"You're just jealous."

"Of what? Your big gay love affair?" Eric snorts. "I'll pass, thanks."

Dylan rolls his eyes as he peers at Eric, looking closer when he sees a spark of something unidentifiable in his eyes. "You *are* jealous!" He holds up a hand to forestall the forthcoming protest. "Not of us," he clarifies with another roll of his eyes. "You're jealous because I'm rooming with Brendan and not with you."

"Like I didn't see *that* coming for the past, I don't know, nine months." Eric turns around, shaking his head. "Trust me, it wasn't a surprise."

"Then what's the issue? And don't tell me nothing," Dylan adds, jabbing his finger into Eric's shoulder and glaring sternly. "You've been moping ever since I picked you up at the airport. Which, by the way, required that Brendan and I get here insanely early so we could unload before I went to get you."

"I feel for you. Really. I do," Eric says dryly, casting a sidelong glance at Dylan. "And I'm not moping."

"Uh-huh."

"I'm *not*."

Dylan narrows his eyes as he looks more closely at his friend. There's something bothering Eric, he knows that much, and he feels as though he should be able to figure out what it is. It takes him a minute, but then it hits him, hard, and his mouth drops open. "You're nervous!"

Now that he's seen it, it's obvious. Eric's feeling the exact same way Dylan was a year ago. It's the most beautiful form of payback Dylan could possibly have imagined, which is ironic, as Dylan decided almost a year ago that Eric didn't deserve payback. Skipping out on last year's Dragon*Con is the best thing Eric has ever done for Dylan.

"I am not!"

"Yes, you are! I can see it! You're worried that you won't get along with Nate!"

"I am not! I just don't know why you're making me room with him. If you had to ditch me, couldn't you have at least hooked me up with one of those girls from your pictures? The red-haired one is *hot*."

"Okay, first of all? No one is *making* you room with anyone. We arranged it when the two of you wouldn't stop moping about not having someone to room with. Second," Dylan continues, ticking the points off on his fingers, "Elisa has a roommate, and I'm pretty sure that if she needed one, she wouldn't want to room with some guy she's never met."

"You're depriving me, Dylan."

"Yeah, whatever. You'll get to meet her, I'm sure. You can flirt all you want then. Just don't tell her I said that," he adds, pointing his finger at Eric and frowning sternly.

"Oh! Do I really have your permission to flirt?" Eric perks up sarcastically, rolling his eyes. "You'd better be glad I love you, bitch. Ditching me to room with your boyfriend and acting like I need your permission to flirt," he mutters, scowling down over the railing toward the floor below.

"Hey, I told you back in May that you could room with us if you really wanted to."

"And then you proceeded to tell me how you would still have sex every night!"

"Not every night," Dylan protests. "Sometimes we'll have it in the morning, or afternoon. Or all three," he finishes, grinning wickedly.

"Dude!" Eric covers his ears and squeezes his eyes shut. "TMI! I am *not* rooming with you. Whatever this Nate guy is like, he can't be worse than that." He shudders dramatically before dropping his hands from his ears.

Dylan grins and leans in close to Eric's ear as soon as his hands fall. "Good, 'cause we got a king-sized bed, and we're going to sleep naked."

"Man!" Eric shudders dramatically. "I did not need to know that! TMI, Dylan! TMI!"

Dylan just laughs and slaps Eric on the shoulder as he turns away. "Come on. They should be here in a few minutes." He heads toward the escalators without waiting for Eric, a wide grin on his face. This year, Dylan can't wait for his roommate to get here from the airport. As soon as he does, it will officially be the start of the Best Dragon*Con Ever.

BRENDAN curses as a crowd of people surges past him, bumping into him with their bags and rolling over his toes with their wheeled luggage. It seems as though this year everyone got the memo they hadn't last year, and every single traveler is in such a hurry to leave the Atlanta airport that they can't be bothered to check for anyone in their way. Brendan isn't a small guy, after all, and he's standing well enough out of the way that it shouldn't be a problem to go around him, and yet half the crowd in baggage claim seems to want to walk right through where he is.

He's going to kill Nate when he gets here.

This year, at least, Brendan got to drive, riding with Dylan from their new house in Rochester, but they'd both felt bad about leaving Eric and Nate hanging after so many years of going to Dragon*Con with them, especially since it was their actions a year ago that led to where they are now. If it hadn't been for Eric and Nate both flaking out on them at the last minute, Brendan never would have met Dylan, so he feels grateful to both of them.

He's just not sure he feels grateful enough to justify two trips to the Atlanta airport in one day.

Unfortunately, their friends hadn't been able to coordinate their flights here, and since neither Dylan nor Brendan felt right expecting them to take the shuttle or MARTA, they'd agreed to pick them both up separately. At least they'll get to drop them off together—though fitting all the luggage in the car will be an interesting experiment—but for now, Brendan is stuck at the airport while Dylan is back at the hotel helping Eric get settled.

At least Nate's flight arrived on time, if the board is to be believed, anyway. Brendan hasn't seen him yet, but it just landed ten minutes ago, and he remembers well how long it took him to disembark and make it to baggage claim last year. The fact that the people already in baggage claim seem to be in a huge hurry to leave the airport doesn't mean that the people Nate will have to navigate around will be, and even if everyone is, it'll still take him a good fifteen or twenty minutes to get off the plane and get through the crowds.

Brendan has time to kill, so he takes a few steps back, leans against the wall, and pulls out his phone. At least he can entertain himself. His LiveJournal and Twitter ought to keep him amused until Nate makes his way to the baggage claim.

He's fully engrossed in the slew of celebrity and news tweets that have gone up since that morning—and thinking that he really needs to follow more people he knows in real life—when Nate stops in front of him, dropping his backpack on Brendan's foot. "Ow!"

"Nice to see you too, asshole."

Brendan rolls his eyes and pulls Nate in for a hug, kicking the backpack off his feet as he moves. "It's only been a week. You can't possibly be pining away for me already."

"Like I would ever pine for you." Nate scoops the backpack up and thrusts it at Brendan. "Here, make yourself useful and hold this while I grab my suitcase."

"I am being useful!" Brendan calls after him. "I picked you up, didn't I?"

"More useful, then!" Nate hollers back. "Since I'm hardly going to get to see you this weekend!"

Brendan just rolls his eyes as he tucks his phone back in his pocket. He's not going to dignify that with a response.

By the time they get out to the car, Nate has regaled Brendan with horror stories of his flight in. Apparently, Brendan's experience last year was calm and peaceful compared to Nate's trip this year. Brendan has trouble believing it, seeing as how Nate arrived on time and Brendan didn't, but he's not going to argue. If Nate wants to moan and bitch about his horrible flight, Brendan will let him. He did make Nate fly instead of riding with him as he had every other year, after all.

It's not until they're pulling onto I-85 that Nate twists sideways in his seat and does his best to catch Brendan's eye. Brendan flicks his gaze over to let him know that he's listening, but doesn't take his eyes off the road for any longer than that. Even in the middle of the afternoon, traffic around downtown Atlanta can be a mess, and Brendan doesn't want to wreck Dylan's car.

"So," Nate says once he knows he has Brendan's attention. "Tell me about this Eric guy."

Brendan shrugs. "I've only met him a couple of times. He's Dylan's friend, the one who ditched him last year so we ended up rooming together."

"You totally owe me for that, by the way."

"You've been saying that for the past year. There's a statute of limitations on these things, you know. I'm not going to owe you forever. And Dylan owes *Eric*," he adds, pointing a finger at Nate. "So don't even go there."

"You hooked me up to room with the guy Dylan owes for your happiness?" Nate cackles, and the sound is so sinister that Brendan can't help but glance over to see the expression he's making. He immediately wishes he hadn't. Nate looks positively evil as he smirks and rubs his hands together in glee.

This cannot be good. "Oh God. Nate, what are you planning?"

"You're just going to have to wait and see." His expression somehow grows even more ominous, and he cackles once again. "This is going to be good."

Somehow, Brendan isn't sure he agrees. It's going to be a very interesting convention.

DYLAN is practically vibrating with excitement when Brendan stops in front of him, grinning widely. He's got a backpack slung over one shoulder, a guitar in one hand, and as he walks in, he keeps glancing behind him to where Nate is dragging a large suitcase. As soon as he sees Dylan, his face breaks out into a wide grin, and he hurries forward, letting the backpack fall to the ground and hugging and kissing Dylan like it's been months since they've seen each other instead of just hours.

"Hey," Dylan whispers when they break apart, his eyes never leaving Brendan's. "Nate get in okay?"

"Yep. Everything's taken care of."

"Good." That means they're free to head down to get their badges and then they can take the car to the MARTA lot. After they spend a little time catching up, of course.

It's a little ridiculous, especially since they've been living together for the past two months—and Dylan still isn't over how excited that makes him—but there's something about being here, at Dragon*Con, that has him giddy with excitement and desperate to spend every possible second pressed tightly against Brendan's side. It's an anniversary, after all, and they get to celebrate with five full days of fun and friends at the place that brought them together.

It's *awesome*.

So awesome, in fact, that Dylan forgets about everyone and everything else until Eric clears his throat, coughing loudly in their ears and startling Dylan enough that he looks away from Brendan. "What?"

"Are the two of you going to just gaze soulfully at each other for the rest of the weekend, or do you think that maybe you could introduce us and help us get his stuff up to our room?"

The first option sounds infinitely better, but since he's a good friend, Dylan sighs dramatically and pushes Eric forward. "Eric, this is Nate. Nate, this is Eric. There," he adds, turning back to his friend. "Now you know each other."

Brendan chuckles as he leans into Dylan's side, Nate's backpack still at his feet. "Eloquent."

"Shut up."

"No, I like it. Short and to the point. Don't tell them anything about each other or make sure neither of them is going to kill the other one. You should hook people up all the time."

"Hey, it's more than we got."

"*We* talked online first. A little bit, anyway. I don't think they've talked at all."

"And yet they seem to be off to a better start than we were. Neither of them looks pissed off yet."

"It's not my fault I was late!"

"It's not *my* fault you couldn't remember to call!"

"I'm not the one who was pissed off for no reason!"

"Yeah, well, I'm not the one who—"

"Guys!" Eric steps in and waves an arm in their faces. "Do we have to rehash this? Again? We all know, you two hated each other at first sight, and now you're sickeningly sweet and happy. We get it; you don't have to go over it *again*."

"You forgot the part where it's all thanks to us."

Eric blinks, looking stunned for a minute, then breaks out into a huge grin. "Oh my God, you're right! I never thought of it that way before. We totally deserve all the credit!"

Nate leans in close, a wicked grin on his face. "You want to help me figure out how to get them to reward us?"

"Um, *duh*." Eric's grin grows to match Nate's. "I'm thinking humiliation. And stuff. I need a new sword."

Dylan manages to pull himself away from Brendan and steps forward, pointing a finger directly in Eric's face. "No. You are *not* getting a new sword."

"Wanna bet?"

It's tempting, but Dylan knows that Eric will buy the sword just to win, so he shakes his head firmly. "I'm not an idiot, Eric. *I* will not buy you a sword. *Neither will Brendan*," he adds quickly when Eric's gaze swings over.

Eric's mouth falls open, but before he can say anything, Nate steps forward and slings an arm around Eric's shoulders. "Come with me, young padawan. I have much to teach you about the art of blackmail."

"It's not—"

Nate puts a finger over Eric's lips, hands him the backpack and guitar case, and leads him off. "Much to learn, have you. Teach you, I will."

Dylan watches them leave with a sinking feeling in his gut. "He's going to do that all weekend, isn't he?"

"Yep." Brendan nods, sighing dramatically as he leans his head against Dylan's shoulder again. "He's going to do his best to drive us insane and humiliate us."

"And Eric will do everything in his power to get us to buy them things." Dylan closes his eyes and lets his head fall forward. "We are so screwed."

Brendan lifts his head, cups Dylan's chin, and pulls him in for a kiss. "Not yet, we're not, but we probably have time before we have to head down to check-in if you want."

Dylan's eyes widen. He hadn't planned to get any time alone with Brendan from the time they picked up Eric until after they'd checked in and were taking the car up to the MARTA lot. The idea that they could make use of this unexpected free time hadn't occurred to him. "We—"

"Eric and Nate seem fine on their own, which gives us"— Brendan looks down at his watch—"about a half an hour to kill. You wanna?"

There's no way they can possibly get to the elevators fast enough to suit Dylan.

THE Peachtree Center food court is crowded when they return from dropping off the car. It's not as packed as it will be tomorrow, but Brendan is glad that they don't have any luggage, because it's crowded enough that trying to navigate through with bags and suitcases would be awkward, and right now, Brendan doesn't want any sort of delays. He has plans, important ones, and he'd really, really like to get started on them.

Dylan cuts deftly through the crowd, leading Brendan out of the station the right way and swinging around the lines gathering at the fast-food places with ease. Not for the first time, Brendan is glad that his boyfriend is as tall and well built as he is. It makes following behind him easy, and he anticipates that this year, he won't have any trouble getting through the crowds to the places he wants to go.

Assuming he sticks with Dylan, of course, which he has every intention of doing. Sure, they'll split up some, to go to different panels and to hang out with their own friends—Brendan plans on keeping Eric and Nate apart as much as possible, thank you—but for the most part, he fully intends to be wherever Dylan is, and he knows Dylan feels the same way about him.

It's going to make for an awesome convention.

When they get back to the Marriott, Dylan stops, leaning against one of the walls near the stairs, and glances at his watch. "We've got twenty minutes. You want to go to the room, or just head to the restaurant?"

Brendan looks across the Atrium Level toward Sear. There are people gathered outside, and though he called and made reservations for tonight earlier in the week, he figures it can't hurt to head on over now. They have a big party, after all, assuming that everyone manages to show up, and if he and Dylan aren't there to coordinate the arrival of all their friends, he's not sure what will happen. "Let's head over."

Disappointment flashes briefly across Dylan's face, and he looks longingly up through the atrium toward their room, but then he smiles and takes a step forward. "Yeah, okay."

"I'll make it up to you later," Brendan promises in a low voice as he falls into step next to Dylan. He would like to head up to their room too, but if they do, they'll probably miss dinner altogether, and he's afraid of what their friends will get up to if they're not there. "I just don't want Nate and Eric to have unimpeded access to anyone else."

"Good call." Dylan laughs, his head thrown back, letting Brendan guide him around the obstacles between them and the restaurant. "We should try to get the girls on our side."

"I dunno. They might really think that those knuckleheads deserve to be rewarded. I know Elisa squealed for a good ten minutes when I told her we were moving in together."

"Kelly did too." Dylan stops just outside the restaurant, standing with his back to the entrance. "I think she was more excited than I was."

Brendan peeks inside, verifying that none of their friends are there yet, and shakes his head. "I don't think I'm *capable* of getting as excited as Elisa got."

"There is that." Dylan ruffles Brendan's hair. "You are a little low-key sometimes. You should work on that."

"Shut up." Brendan shoves at Dylan's chest. "I am not."

"Are so."

"Am not!" He dodges as Dylan tries to ruffle his hair again. "And stop that, you evil brat!"

"I'm not evil!"

"You are too!"

Dylan pauses, thinking about that for a moment. "Yeah, all right. Maybe sometimes. But you love me anyway."

Brendan's heart melts again, and he's not sure if it's from the words, Dylan's sweet smile, or something else entirely. "Yeah, I do," he admits softly, grinning as he steps a little bit closer to his partner.

Dylan's whole demeanor softens as his smile grows. "I know. I love you too." He slips his arm over Brendan's shoulder, pulling him close, and kisses him softly.

Brendan returns the kiss, sliding his arm around Dylan's waist and putting his other hand on Dylan's chest, his palm pressed over Dylan's heart. When they break apart, he fingers the rainforest jasper stone in the necklace that still hangs there and smiles at the bracelet on his own wrist, marveling at how well they complement each other and grinning wider as he remembers the night they gave the jewelry to each other.

He's still standing there, tucked under Dylan's arm with his hand pressed to Dylan's chest, when Kevin and Laura arrive, grinning widely and waving madly from across the hotel. Dylan waves back, but Brendan stays exactly where he is, tucked close to Dylan and marveling at the steady beat of his lover's heart under his palm.

As his friends arrive, laughing and joking and teasing them, all Brendan can think is that this year is going to be the best Dragon*Con ever.

He has Dylan.

NESSA L. WARIN lives in southwestern Ohio and enjoys reading, wine tastings, and watching fantasy movies and television. She also participates in roleplaying events and can be found running around in costume during at least one Renaissance festival and one fantasy convention a year.

When she's not playing, Nessa works in the corporate office of a large life insurance company coordinating the production and mailing of marketing materials. She shares her home with a cat that enjoys getting in the way when she's trying to write and owns far more books than she really has room to keep.

DREAMLANDS

FELICITAS IVEY

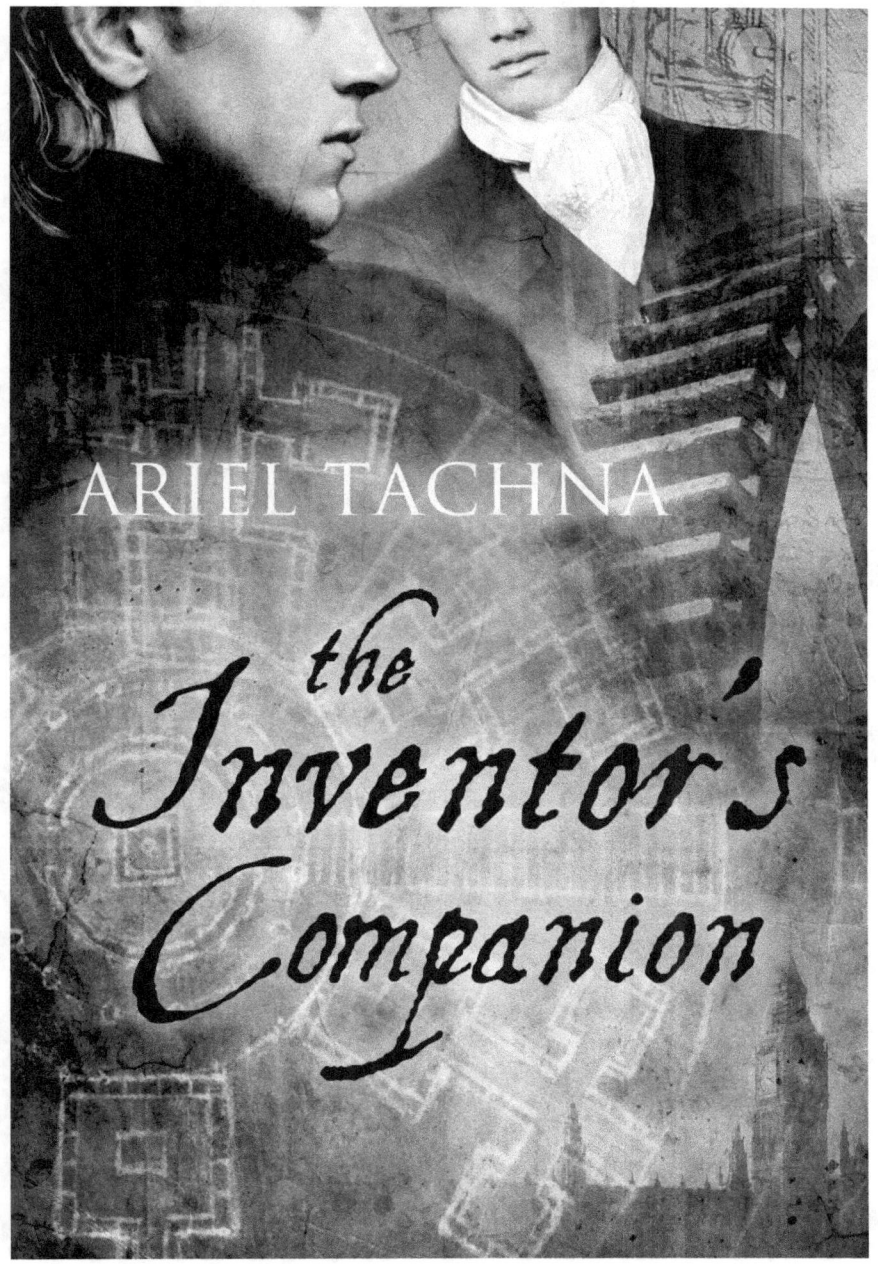

ARIEL TACHNA

the Inventor's Companion

Also from DREAMSPINNER PRESS

http://www.dreamspinnerpress.com